PRAISE FOR
COURT OF FOXES

… a powerful and dramatic piece of writing that has all
the ingredients necessary to appeal to both young and old
readers alike.
Phil Carradice

Court of Foxes uses legend and magic to tell a really exciting
story.
Elizabeth Arnold

… most intriguing, full of action, [...] an excellent balance
between narrative and dialogue.
Valerie Wilding

COURT

OF

FOXES

BRIAN LUX

Copyright © Brian Lux 2008
Cover Art © Helen Lake, Helen Lake Fine Arts 2008
Cover Design by Discovered Authors

This first edition published in Great Britain in 2008 by
DA Diamonds – a Discovered Authors' imprint

The right of Brian Lux to be identified as the Author of the
Work has been asserted by him in accordance with the Copyright,
Designs and Patent Act 1988

A CIP catalogue record for this book is available
from the British Library.

ISBN 978-1-906146-74-0

Available from Discovered Authors Online –
All major online retailers and available to order through all UK bookshops

Or contact:

Books
Discovered Authors
Roslin Road, London
W3 8DH

0844 800 5214
books@discoveredauthors.co.uk
www.discoveredauthors.co.uk

Printed in the UK by BookForce International

BookForce International
Roslin Road, London
W3 8DH
www.bookforce.co.uk

Acknowledgements

The staff at Llandudno Library for their help in Welsh translation.

Byron Rogers (The Traveller), whose intriquing article in Saga magazine gave me the inspiration for my story.

Finally, my long suffering wife, Gale, for her support and encouragement in my writing endeavours.

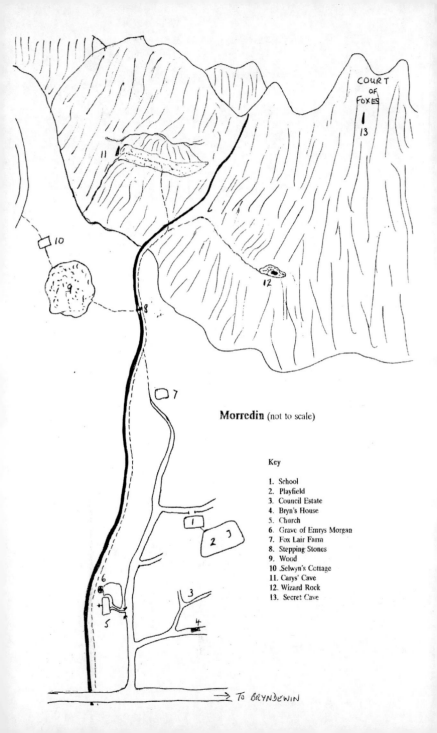

COURT OF FOXES

13

12

10

9

8

7

Morredin (not to scale)

Key

1. School
2. Playfield
3. Council Estate
4. Bryn's House
5. Church
6. Grave of Emrys Morgan
7. Fox Lair Farm
8. Stepping Stones
9. Wood
10. Selwyn's Cottage
11. Carys' Cave
12. Wizard Rock
13. Secret Cave

11

1

2

3

6

5

3

4

→ TO BRYNDEWIN

CHAPTER ONE

The man threw back the hood of his black cloak, dark eyes glittering with excitement. Walking towards the star-shaped flat stone on the hillside, he clutched a leather book tightly.

Placing the book carefully on the stone, he took out a key ring from a pocket in his cloak. It held seven gold keys. The time had come.

'Adentium, mesantium, nostrarium,' he shouted to the darkening sky, his arms outstretched. An answering rumble of thunder bounced off the hillside as he opened the first lock on the book.

In the villages below, dogs howled and shivered. People hurried indoors and crossed themselves as they looked fearfully towards the hills known as the 'Court of Foxes'.

'Dyn Hysbys,' they whispered. 'The Wise Man prays.'

Bryn strode along the country lane deep in thought. Once again, sleep had been disturbed by the same nightmare. He shivered as he recalled the details that had woken him sweating with fright. He'd bitten his blankets to stop himself screaming.

He was in a dark cave, and it was cold. The dampness

enveloped him in an icy cloak. His hands reached out to feel the slippery wet stone. Water dripped off the ceiling. As he peered through the gloom, he could see a faint glow in a distant tunnel. Something told him there was danger ahead. He could smell it, a stomach-turning stench of something rotting. He knew that he had to continue the journey, there was no turning back. Picking his way over the uneven path, he headed towards the tunnel.

Icy water dripped onto him from the small stalactites on the roof. Heart pounding with fear, he was suddenly hurtled from his dream back into his bed. But each time the dream returned, Bryn went a little further on his journey.

Walking to the banks of a chuckling stream that meandered through the fields, he sat down and stared into the clear water. He wanted to think. Why was he in that cave being half scared to death? There must be a reason. He couldn't tell the grown-ups. Granddad would only tell him to 'grow up'. He was always telling him that life was harder when he was his age. What did he know? He was ancient.

'Something troubles you, young man. I see it in your face.'

Bryn turned his head, and the hairs stood up on the back of his neck. Looking down at him was a vision from medieval times. He stared at the tall figure dressed in a dark brown parka and well-worn faded blue jeans. The hood was thrown back off the head to reveal a mop of thick tousled white hair, matched by a luxurious bushy white beard. His fear receded as his gaze met that of the old man. The blue eyes, set in a lined face, had wisdom in their depths and a friendly twinkle.

'Who are you?' whispered Bryn.

'Selwyn, and I've not seen you around these parts.' He used a staff held in his right hand to slowly sit down on the grass.

'We've only just come to live here,' said Bryn, and thought

splashed water over his hands. He made loud noises as he cupped water over his face and mouth. The towel was used vigorously then he walked back.

'Soap,' ordered Gareth from behind the newspaper.

Bryn pulled a face before retracing his steps. He used the soap liberally before rinsing his hands and sitting down again. He stared at the newspaper in front of his grandfather's face.

'Met a strange man today,'

'What do you mean by "strange"?'

'He looked like a monk.'

'Why a monk?' said Bryn's mother, carrying a steaming pot of vegetables. She placed them on a raised iron plate in the centre of the table.

'Well he did, dressed in a brown jacket thing with a hood. Had a mass of white hair and a bushy beard.' Bryn grinned. 'He'd make a smashing Father Christmas.'

His grandfather slowly folded his newspaper and walked from the table to the Welsh dresser, where he put it down. He turned round and looked first at Bryn then his mother. In a quivering voice, Gareth spoke in Welsh to her.

'What's he saying, Mum?'

'Can't understand it all, but it's something to do with that man you met.'

'You're not to talk to that man again, Bryn,' said his grandfather. 'He's bad. Better to keep away from him.'

'I thought he was friendly once we got talking.'

'I'm not saying any more, Bryn, but I think it best if you forget him.'

Bryn opened his mouth to reply, but a fierce glance from his grandfather made it clear there would be no further discussion. He watched his mother return with a pan of lamb chops. She flashed him a smile as she doled out the meal and he quietly ate his food.

Mum's a fantastic cook, he thought, and stole a glance at his grandfather. He couldn't understand why he should be so adamant that the strange man he'd met should be forgotten. As he chewed the tender lamb meat, Bryn thought again about Selwyn. No, there was nothing bad about the old man. Odd maybe, but definitely not bad.

Bryn yawned as he settled down in bed. It had been a great day, tiring but exciting. Now he had his own dog, but still hadn't thought of a name. As he let names trickle through his tired mind, he closed his eyes and let sleep embrace him, followed by the recurring dream.

Once again he was treading carefully along the dank slippery path. His nightmare was vivid as he threshed in bed, head jerking from side to side in his desperation to wake up. He didn't want to continue on that frightening journey. He wanted to be back in reality, warmth and safety. As the narrow tunnel reached a right hand turn, Bryn was conscious of a presence hidden from view where the path disappeared. He couldn't see anything but could sense something…or somebody.

'I don't want to go on,' he cried in his sleep. 'I want to go home.' But a hard menacing voice ordered him to continue. It seemed to come from round the corner.

Bryn saw his dog in the distance, and called to him. He called louder and louder until he was awake and shouting at the top of his voice.

'Cadno, come here! Help me, Cadno!' yelled Bryn, sitting up in bed and staring into the darkness.

Lights came on in the cottage, and as the dog barked in the kitchen, Bryn's mother ran from her room.

'What's the matter?' she asked, sitting on his bed and holding him close.

'Bad dream.'

the stranger looked like Father Christmas, with his white hair and the beard almost hiding his mouth.

'Ah, yes,' said Selwyn. 'I've heard of your coming. Bryn Mitchell, isn't it? Just you and your mother. Been here about two months.'

'Yes, sir,' said Bryn, and feeling more relaxed, told Selwyn that his mother was Welsh and had come back to her parents' home in the village of Morredin during the summer holidays.

'Only Granddad is still alive.'

'And your father?'

'Dunno where he is,' said Bryn. 'Mum divorced him "cos they were always arguing over him getting drunk.'

'That is sad.'

'Is it? He'd come home stinking drunk, then would go round the house shouting and smashing things.' Bryn shrugged his shoulders. 'Anyway, most of my mates at my old school had divorced parents.'

'So what does your mother do?'

'She's a nurse, and works at the hospital in Bryn... something or other.'

'BrynDewin,' smiled Selwyn. 'And you like your grandfather?'

'He's okay,' said Bryn. 'He's always talking to his friends in Welsh, and it's weird to listen to. Tries it on Mum, but she finds it hard to understand. It's been years since she lived in Wales.' He flashed a brief smile at Selwyn. 'They teach it at school, and the teachers do their best to help me. Reckon they're going to fail. I've only been going a few weeks. Can't see the point of learning it'

Selwyn looked at the gurgling water as he fingered a gold ornament that dangled from a gold chain round his neck.

'It's...' He gazed at Bryn and changed his reply. 'But that

is not what torments you, is it?'

'No.'

'Then tell me all,' said Selwyn. 'There is a saying, which I believe, and it is this: "A trouble shared is a trouble halved."'

Bryn closed his eyes and his voice shook as he relived the terror in his nightmare, and the journey he had to take even though it was frightening.

When the story was finished Selwyn said quietly, 'When did this dream begin?'

'When we moved here.'

'How often does it come?'

'It was only once every week or so, but now it's most nights. I'm scared to go to sleep.' Bryn's heart raced. 'Do you think it's got something to do with us coming here?'

'I think it very likely that is the truth of the matter,' said Selwyn, fingering the gold chain.

'Why should living here give me bad dreams?'

'Strange things have happened here since time began. Powerful forces abide in these parts, some good, some bad,' said Selwyn. 'Have you told your mother?'

Bryn shook his head. 'Mum would laugh at me.'

'Don't,' said Selwyn. The sharp tone of his voice made Bryn jerk upright.

'It is best that few know of your secret.' The old man stood up and, grasping his staff, swept it round the scene. 'I believe you are here for a purpose. What it is, I do not yet know.' He placed his free hand on Bryn's shoulder. 'But I will find out and tell you.' Turning on his heel, he strode rapidly away.

'When will I see you again?' shouted Bryn, but Selwyn disappeared over the top of the bank. Only the cries of birds and the babble of the stream answered.

* * *

Where have you been?' said Bryn's grandfather.

'Out,' said Bryn, he walked over to the kitchen table and reached for an apple from the fruit bowl.

'That's no answer.' Gareth Powell's voice still had the sharpness of a man who had been a career soldier. Bryn stared at his grandfather before biting a chunk from his apple.

'Sorry, Granddad,' he mumbled as he chewed. Seeing the warning glare in Gareth's eyes he finished the mouthful before continuing. 'Went down to the stream to think.'

'Think about what?'

'Rather not say,' said Bryn, then frowned as he looked round the kitchen. 'Where's Mum?'

'She'll not be long. Just went back to town to get some more shopping.'

Bryn wandered out and stood by the gate, munching his apple. He watched the birds wheeling in the sky. The distant hills, bathed in sunshine, looked bleak and hostile. A tooting of a horn jerked him out of his daydream, and he grinned as his mother's small red car ground to a halt by the cottage. She waved, and leaving the car opened the rear door. Reaching inside, she emerged with a small black and brown dog at the end of a lead.

'What do you think?' she asked, as the dog raced forwards to try and reach Bryn. Its tail wagged furiously as it barked madly.

'Crazy,' said Bryn and knelt down and closed his eyes as a long pink tongue washed his face. He stroked the small head and felt the soft velvety ears. 'Where did you get it?'

'Heard about it from a patient at the hospital,' said Mum. 'Incidentally, "it" is a "him". Anyway, the poor little fellow was found running round the hospital grounds. Probably dumped by his owners.' She looked into Bryn's questioning eyes. 'People do that, Bryn. Get a dog for a present, then get bored and dump it, like so much rubbish.' She gave the lead to Bryn then reached for the shopping. 'Take him inside.'

'What about Granddad?'

'If you really want to know, it was your grandfather who suggested I bring the dog home. He's not as stuffy as you think, young man.'

'What are we going to call him?'

'You decide. He's your dog.'

'Mine?'

'That's right. Now take him while I go and get supper ready.'

'Come on, dog,' said Bryn, and the newcomer to the Powell household bounded after him as they wandered into a field behind the cottage.

'What am I going to call you?' said Bryn as he watched the dog race round the field. 'It's not going to be easy, 'cos it must be something special. It's got to be a name no other dog in the whole world has ever been called.' He noticed that the ears were long and pointed, standing erect. The cheeks had white patches, and the paws seemed much too large for such a small animal.

'You're a funny looking dog,' said Bryn. 'Look more like a fox, but it doesn't matter. I'm sure we'll be great pals.'

'Supper's ready,' called his mother, and Bryn walked slowly back to the cottage. He gave a final pat to his pet and watched his mother make him lie down in a basket.

'Smells great,' said Bryn, closing his eyes and breathing deeply the delicious aromas wafting from the kitchen. He walked to the kitchen table, pulled out a chair and sat down.

'What?' he said, seeing the accusing gaze of his grandfather, as he slowly lowered his newspaper.

'Haven't you forgotten something?'

'Don't think so.'

'In this house, we wash our hands before eating.'

'Sorry, Granddad,' said Bryn, rushing to the sink where he

The children yelled and jumped up to try and catch the ball. Bryn saw the ball curling down towards him and reached out. An elbow was dug into his ribs and he gasped before collapsing in a heap. Other children collided with each other, and stumbled over his prostrate form. Chaos reigned, and the teacher frantically blew his whistle as the laughing, yelling pupils disentangled themselves.

Bryn rolled over on to his stomach, and bent his knees under himself. His ribs ached where the elbow had dug in. He heard someone lean down and yell something in his ear, but could not understand as it was spoken in Welsh.

As he forced himself to his feet, Bryn wondered if the elbowing had been an accident. He had doubts, which were reinforced by the grins cast in his direction and the whispered comments between pupils.

'We'll try it one more time,' said Hugh, and looked at Bryn who was clutching his side. 'Are you all right?'

'Yes, sir,'

'You can rest if you want to.'

Bryn looked at the other children. All eyes were on him, waiting for an answer. He guessed they would not be expecting him to continue. I'll show them. I'll show them that we are just as tough in England.

'Thank you, sir, but I'd like to carry on.'

'Good lad. I think we'll try to kick drop goals over the bar,' said the teacher. 'I don't think any of you should get hurt.' He glared at Carys. 'Even if some of you have other ideas. Now I know this is a football goal, but just imagine that long poles reach up at each end of the cross bar.'

Bryn was surprised when Hugh took the ball, lumbered forwards, and dropped the ball to his feet before neatly kicking it over the bar. As the children clapped, he beamed with pleasure, then gave the ball to a boy. Applause gave way to laughter as the erstwhile rugby player missed and fell over.

Hugh beckoned to Bryn who caught the ball then stood, motionless, in the centre of the field. He was still feeling the ache from the elbowing but a mischievous idea was forming in his head.

'Come on Bryn, let's try and make a rugby player of you.'

Bryn stared at the teacher, then at the children. They'll be expecting me to make a complete fool of myself, he thought. Maybe I'll just show them what a real game is like.

He placed the ball on the ground and tapped it forward. The oval ball rolled to one side, and Bryn trotted forwards tapping it gently in front of him. One boy ran towards him, and Bryn neatly swerved sending the boy sprawling in the wrong direction.

As he gathered pace, the other children decided to join in and tried to tackle him or kick the ball away from his feet.

'This is a rugby lesson, boy,' shouted Hugh, 'not your damned soccer.'

Oh no, it isn't, thought Bryn, tapping the ball between the feet of an advancing Carys. He ran round her and kicked the ball towards the goal. It bounced awkwardly away from the arms of another boy. Bryn raced to the ball, and as it bounced off the grass, kicked it squarely into the open goal.

'Yes!' he yelled, punching the air with one fist. 'Come on, the Rams!'

He turned round, face beaming with pleasure, then picked up the ball and ran with it to the teacher.

'That's the football I like, sir.'

'Maybe, Bryn,' sighed Hugh, taking the ball. 'But in the meantime, can we practise drop kicks?' He pointed to another boy who took the ball and just shaved the top of the cross bar with his kick.

'Who are the Rams?' said Gwyn.

'Derby County. Best team in England.'

'Better than Man United?'

'Maybe second best.'

A light breeze rustled the trees at the edge of the playing field, and Bryn watched several birds hurtle from the branches and fly upwards into the sky. Their cries were loud, and agitated as though something had frightened them.

As he wandered over for a closer look, something caught his eye at the base of the trees, and his heart lurched. A brown fox trotted out and sat on the grass, staring at him. Bryn mouthed something and tried to attract the attention of Gwyn.

'What is it?' said Gwyn, ambling over as he saw Bryn waving madly.

'Can you see that fox?'

'What fox?'

'That one over there,' said Bryn turning to point at the trees.

'You're imagining things. That's a rabbit.'

Bryn stared at the rabbit sitting on the grass washing its face and ears. He knew there had been a fox. He had not imagined the brown animal, sitting by the trees, almost smiling at him. Maybe it was best to keep his thoughts to himself.

'You're probably right. I seem to have foxes on the brain. Let's get back to the others.'

Gwyn was silent as he followed Bryn back to the other children who were still kicking the rugby ball mostly under the cross bar.

CHAPTER FIVE

B ryn ambled along with the other children from school, after changing into their day clothes. He had tried to get into the spirit of Rugby, but knew that it would never replace soccer in his heart. He kicked a stone in anger as he remembered life in Derby, and when spotted by scouts for the 'Rams.' Who knows where it could have lead, he thought. He imagined leading out the first team to the roars of the crowd.

He looked at the winding road, and the packed houses and cottages. No chance of getting spotted by anybody here, in this dump.

'You did quite a good drop goal in the end,' said Carys, 'for a boy.'

'I'd like to see a girl hammering in one past a diving goalie.'

'You should have seen Farty's face when you kicked it in,' said Gwyn.

Bryn grinned. 'It would be a joke seeing him try and dribble past a defender. Probably fall over his feet.'

As they wandered into the main street, Gwyn glanced to his right and pointed out a figure coming towards them.

'It's the mad monk. Hope he doesn't want to speak to us.

'Just walk past, and say nothing,' snapped Carys, and increased her step.

'Isn't that Selwyn?' said Bryn, recognising the brown coat and the bushy white beard of the old man.

'He's the "mad monk", and we don't speak to him,' said Carys. 'And if you've any sense, you won't either.'

'Why not?' said Bryn, returning the wave of Selwyn. 'Met him a few days ago, and had a chat.'

'What about?' said Carys. The accusation in her voice, and the cold expression in her eyes, worried Bryn. What's it to do with her, he thought.

'This and that,' he said, and left the group as the old man beckoned him. He felt the stares of the children burning into his back as he walked across the road.

'And how has the day been for you, young Bryn?' said Selwyn.

'So, so. We had sports afternoon today.'

'That is very acceptable, Bryn. Much better than lessons, surely?' The old man turned on his heel and began to walk away towards a gate at the far end of the road. It led to a path that wound its way across several fields to the distant hills.

'Trouble is, old Farty was trying to teach us rugby, and I want to play football.' Bryn found himself trotting to keep up with the long strides of Selwyn.

'Am I correct in thinking this 'old Farty' is Mr Price, your teacher?'

'Yes, and the joke is he doesn't seem to know when he does it.'

'When I was your age, respect for teachers and our parents governed our lives.' Selwyn sighed. He gazed at the fields, and the hills rising in the distance, bathed in sunshine.

'Your teacher might be a little large now…'

'He's fat, not just large.'

39

'Maybe,' nodded Selwyn. 'But he was a young man once, very fit, and a Welsh Rugby schoolboy international player.'

'You're having me on.'

'No, young Bryn, I am not "having you on", as you say.' He leaned against the gate and looked back at the village. 'You must never believe everything you see for the first time, nor what you are told about people.' He grasped his staff firmly, and his beard shook with emotion as he spoke.

'Don't understand.'

'Bryn, I tell you this, for your own good.' Selwyn paused then placed a hand gently on his shoulder. 'This place is a good example of what I mean. It is not all that you might see at first sight. There are secrets here.'

'What secrets?'

'I'll say no more for now.' Selwyn looked across the road. 'You had better go. Your friends are waiting for you.'

Bryn opened his mouth to speak but Selwyn had turned away and was opening the gate to cross the field.

As the old man strode quickly along the worn path, Bryn ran back to the other children who were watching him approach. Their silence was disturbing as they stared. He wasn't sure if there was hostility or puzzlement in their gaze.

'What did he want?' said Carys.

'Nothing much.'

'You talked a lot about "nothing much".'

'If you really want to know,' said Bryn, feeling angry at the cross- examination, 'he asked about school, and…' He turned to Gwyn. 'Did you know Mr Price was an international rugby player as a schoolboy?'

'That was centuries ago. Can't imagine him as a schoolboy.'

'What else did he say to you?'

'Nothing,' said Bryn, turning his head quickly from the accusing eyes of Carys.

'As I said, Bryn. It's best you don't speak to him again.'

'He's weird,' said Gwyn.

'There's stories about him,' said another boy.

'What stories?'

'You'll hear about them in time,' said Carys. 'If you saw where he lived, you'd understand why he's called "the mad monk".'

'What's wrong with it?'

'I'm not saying any more, but if he invites you there, don't go.'

Bryn saw the other children nod their agreement, and the conversation quickly switched to the evening's television programme.

The children gradually left the group until there was just Carys and Bryn. They walked in silence, and Bryn stared ahead, aware that Carys stole the occasional glance at him.

'Not angry, are you?'

'A bit,' said Bryn. 'Don't like being told who I can be friends with. Had enough of that when Dad lived with us. That and his temper.'

'Bad was it?'

'He was… impossible when drunk, and that was most nights.'

'Is that why your mother brought you back here?'

'Partly, and partly 'cos he just vanished one night and never came home again.' Bryn smiled briefly at Carys. 'Truth is, I think Mum was glad. Leastwise she never cried, and I'd hear her singing in the kitchen. Anyway, what's your family like?'

'Nothing special. They go back a long time. Both their parents have lived here, and for years and years before that. So we're very, very Welsh.'

'Carys,' said Bryn, as something Selwyn said entered his thoughts. 'What's so special about this place?'

'Special?'

41

'Selwyn told me there are secrets here.'

Carys forced a smile. 'Told you, Bryn, he's mad, and you musn't believe anything he says. As for secrets, there aren't any. You've been here long enough to know that not much happens.'

'Bit of a dump isn't it? Don't know how you stand living here.' Bryn kicked an empty plastic bottle in the air and watched it sail over a wall into the churchyard.

He reddened as two villagers glared at him as they passed. Hearing them talk rapidly in Welsh, he guessed they were making comments about him, and ran into the church grounds. Passing under the lychgate, he quickly read the name of the Minister. The Reverend Broderick Lloyd MA sounded an impressive, fierce member of the clergy.

Treading carefully between the gravestones, he saw the bottle and knelt down to retrieve it. It lay across a grave where the headstone, weather beaten over the years, was eroded with the inscription barely visible. Bryn could just make out the date, 23 July 1896.

Grabbing the bottle, he stood up and looked around. The graveyard extended to two sides of the church, and many headstones were toppled to the ground. Others stood at odd angles, but the harsh winter weather had taken its toll of the stone. He walked between the graves, seeing some of the engraved dates going back much further than 1896.

The setting sun cast shadows among the graves, and the old church looked peaceful. Its walls were local stone, each slab lovingly placed by craftsmen resulting in a colourful mosaic. The roof contrasted with its covering of blue slate tiles, and the heavy wooden door was a feature with two heavy iron hinges.

Bryn crunched his way along the path that skirted the church, past the graveyard, not knowing why. Something made him explore further. He was puzzled by the urge to walk round the churchyard.

Even though his grandfather was a member of the congregation, he and his mother had not been to a service. His parents had never belonged to a church in Derby, and most of his friends never attended services on Sundays.

'Have you found it?' said Carys, running along the path to join him.

'Yes,' said Bryn and waved the plastic bottle.

'Let's go then.'

'In a minute,' said Bryn. 'There's something about this place I can't understand.'

'Nothing special about this place. My parents come here, and so do I.' Carys looked at Bryn. 'Not seen you here, but your granddad's a member, isn't he?'

Bryn nodded and walked to the edge of the graveyard as though impelled by a force. A light breeze ruffled the grass and he scanned the edge of the church grounds, then frowned. He shaded his eyes from the sun and stared ahead.

As his eyes focussed on the ground between two trees, he whispered, 'Isn't that a gravestone over there?'

'Could be,' said Carys quickly, then turned on her heel. 'Come on Bryn, let's go.' She ran away from the church and left the grounds.

Bryn gave a backward glance as he ran after her then grabbed her arm. She halted and snapped, 'What?'

'That was a grave I saw. Nothing "could be", about it. So who is it, and why was he buried away from everyone else?'

'I don't know. Does it matter?'

'That's what's weird. I have this feeling it does.'

Carys grinned. 'And we think the mad monk's weird.'

Bryn dropped the bottle into a waste bin. 'Maybe you're right. It's this place getting to me.'

'If you want to see somewhere really odd, then I'll take you to the mines at Twyn. It's spooky in there, full of ghosts.'

Bryn continued to chat to Carys as they walked, then waved goodbye as she crossed the road. He watched her greet another girlfriend and continue to her home in the Council estate.

Cadno greeted him enthusiastically as he opened the gate of the cottage, and bounded round the garden. The foxy head of the dog brought back images of the distant grave. Bryn found himself puzzling about the identity of the occupant and the reason why it had been placed away from the other graves at the extremity of the church grounds. There had to be a reason and there was something else. He was sure Carys not only knew about the grave, but who was in it. So why did she not want to talk about it?

As he lay in a bath, soaking in the hot water and watching the rising steam mist over the mirror on the wall, Bryn resolved to find out more.

'Judging from the state of your kit you were wrestling in the mud,' said his mother, as she opened the door and entered, carrying a bath towel.

'It was Carys. She did a proper tackle on me.'

'Tough, is she?'

'Not really,' said Bryn. He slowly lowered his head under water, blew some bubbles, then surfaced. 'Mum, do you know something?'

'Know what?'

'Whose grave is that in the church? It's right at the far end of the grounds. I'm sure Carys knows, but she wasn't saying.'

'No idea, but I'll ask your grandfather when I go down.' She placed the towel on a bath stool, then left saying, 'Don't be long, supper's nearly ready.'

Bryn reluctantly stood up and stepped out of the bath. As he towelled himself, he heard his mother knock on the door.

'Supper's in five minutes, Bryn.'

'Did you ask Granddad?'

'Yes.'

'What did he say?'

'Dewin.'

'Whose that?'

'Not "who", but "what", It's welsh for a wizard.'

'Wizard?' said Bryn, and stopped drying himself. 'But didn't he have a name?'

'Your granddad didn't say. In fact he said he wasn't prepared to discuss it further. So take my advice, Bryn and don't ask him.'

Bryn listened to his mother walk down the stairs, and poured talc liberally over himself. Maybe Carys did think him weird, but there was something very weird going on in Morredin, and he was determined to find out.

Hey, he thought, maybe this dump might not be such a dump after all. Maybe there was a mystery to be solved, and he knew just the man to help him.

If anyone knew the identity of the wizard, it would be Selwyn.

CHAPTER SIX

Cadno raced over the springy grass, barking madly. He pushed his nose into a thick clump, flushed out a rabbit, and happily chased it. Bryn laughed as the animal did a sudden right angle turn at the stream bank, and hurtle to freedom. Cadno, not being so agile, fell into the water and emerged, shaking himself vigorously. His ears and tail drooped as though he knew he had been beaten.

'Serves you right, you stupid dog,' said Bryn and was rewarded with a spray of water as Cadno resumed his shaking.

'Keep away,' yelled Bryn. 'You're soaking me.'

Cadno, tail wagging, jumped up at Bryn, shaking himself happily. His young master's jeans were soon damp.

The clear babbling water glistened in the sun, and Bryn was pleased the weekend had brought a break from school. Carys had refused to discuss the remote grave. He decided not to tell her of his awareness it contained the body of a wizard.

Bryn glanced across the stream to the other side. The grassy bank stretched backwards to a hillock, with bushes and a wood that reached to the skyline. Packed trees rose straight and tall, reaching for the blue sky. Cadno halted and gazed at the wood, with erect ears and quivering tail.

'What have you heard,' said Bryn, kneeling down and stroking his dog. 'I can't hear a thing.' He tried to look in the same direction as Cadno, but nothing disturbed the tranquillity of the scene. A light breeze rustled the tops of the trees, and the sheep continued to graze.

'We'll cross over and explore that wood if you want.' Bryn began to follow the stream, looking for somewhere to cross, then halted, as two figures emerged from the wood.

Selwyn was easily recognised, but the slimmer person by his side was not so obvious. When he turned his face to stare at him, Bryn was surprised. He did not expect Idris to be a companion of the 'mad monk'.

'Hi,' yelled Bryn and jumped up and down.

Selwyn waved his staff, and carefully picked his way across the water over some conveniently placed large stones. Idris waited until Selwyn had crossed, then ran to the bank and leapt high in the air, landing near Bryn.

'Nothing to it,' said Idris. He placed his hands on his hips and faced Bryn. 'Bet you can't jump over.'

'No problem.'

Idris smiled. 'Show me then.'

'Right,' said Bryn and walked to the bank. It's not that wide, he thought. All that football training back in Derby has given me speed and strength. But they don't know that. I'll show Idris.

He turned round, walked steadily back then stopped and turned to face the stream. His eyes hardened with concentration. One last deep breath, and he began running, faster and faster, until his right foot pushed him off the bank.

Bryn soared upwards then landed on all fours on the other side. He pushed himself upright, then turned round, raising a clenched fist in victory. Cadno rushed forwards, barking madly, hurling himself across to join his young master.

Idris slowly clapped and began walking away. He stopped, spun on his heels and shouted, 'Well done, now let's see you jump back.'

'No way,' said Bryn and ran to the stepping stones, which Selwyn had used. He carefully walked across the stream while Cadno, still barking happily, splashed through the water.

Reaching Selwyn, Bryn saw Idris break into a trot and run away along the path. So he doesn't want to talk, suits me.

'He's not very friendly, is he?'

'Idris does not have a happy home life. It makes him seem hard and looking for trouble.' Selwyn watched Cadno rolling in the grass, then get up and bark at some birds. 'As I have said before, it is not wise to judge anything, or anybody by first impressions.' He pointed his staff at the dog. 'Anyone seeing him from a distance would think he was a fox.'

'That's his name.'

'Fox?'

'No, Cadno.'

'Cadno?' Selwyn's voice shook. 'Why did you call him that?'

'It happened the first night mum brought him home. Had one of my bad dreams, and I woke calling for him by that name. It was granddad who told me what it meant.' He looked at the old man who was leaning heavily on his staff. 'He was as surprised as you, 'cos I'd never heard the word before.'

'What do you know about foxes here?'

'Only what Carys and Gwyn told me.'

'And what would that be?'

Bryn thought for a moment. 'There used to be lots of foxes round here, years and years ago, but they all suddenly left.'

'Carys is a strange child.' Selwyn knelt down and rubbed

behind Cadno's ears. The dog responded by turning his head and licking the old man's hand. Selwyn was quiet for some time, then looked up at Bryn.

'And did she tell you why they left?'

'No,' said Bryn. 'I do remember something else. She said there was a king of the foxes, but I didn't believe that. Knew it was just made up.'

'There is much you have to learn about Morredin, Bryn, but I think you have to find out for yourself.' Selwyn grunted as he stood up. 'You will recall that at our very first meeting I told you I believed you were here for a purpose.'

Bryn jogged to keep up with Selwyn who strode quickly along the path. He was mumbling to himself, and occasionally shaking his head.

'Did you know the others call you "the mad monk"?'

Selwyn allowed himself a ghost of a smile. 'Oh yes, I've been called that by their parents.'

'Are you a real monk? I don't think you're mad though. Bit odd maybe.'

'And what do you think is a monk, young Bryn?'

'Dunno. Someone who's a bit weird like you I suppose, and lives with other monks.'

'Truth is, a monk belongs to some religious order and usually lives in a monastery. Well, I don't belong to any particular religious group, and I live by myself.' He smiled at his companion. 'So, taking everything together, I cannot be called a monk. No, I am definitely not a monk. As for being mad, you must judge for yourself.'

'Have you always had a big white beard? I mean, you could always get a job as Father Christmas.'

'It is a long story, but all you need to know is I left the world, as you know it, to wander round the country. I came here, a few years ago, and realised there was something very odd, and…'

'What was odd?'

Selwyn stopped and fingered his gold ornament. 'I would rather not discuss it at the moment, Bryn, if you don't mind. Let me just say that I knew I should stay here. My presence and my beliefs were needed in Morredin.'

'I knew it,' said Bryn. 'There is something odd. It might be a dump of a place, but there's strange things here.' He tugged Selwyn's sleeve. 'Do you know anything about that weird grave in the churchyard?'

'Possibly.'

'Then who is it, and why is it well away from the others?'

'All in good time, Bryn. All in good time.'

'Then why did my granddad call him the wizard?'

'Maybe,' said Selwyn quietly, 'because he was a wizard.' He ruffled Bryn's head. 'Of course, that was a long time ago. Long before I was even born, and you must know that stories abound in these parts. Anyway, time I went. Much to do. So I will say "adieu". That's French for 'goodbye', incidentally.'

'Can we meet again, soon?' said Bryn.

'Of course.' Selwyn increased his stride and was soon back at the stepping stones. As he carefully crossed, he stood in the middle and shouted, 'We have much to talk about, and you have much to learn.'

Bryn watched the old man cross and walk across the field to the wood and disappear.

'Tell you what, Cadno. I think he knows all about that person in the grave. Looks like I'll just have to find out myself. No one's going to talk about it.'

Cadno listened, his head tilted to one side. As Bryn finished speaking, the dog barked and darted away.

A distant rumble of thunder made Bryn look skywards. The air was still, and although he was in the sun, the skyline was black and moving quickly down the hill. Another rumble rolled round the hills, then an ominous silence.

'Better get home quickly before we get soaked,' said Bryn and retraced his steps.

The sun gradually disappeared behind thickening clouds, and a chill permeated the air. Bryn shivered and began to run.

As he ran, fear enveloped him. He looked round and could not rid himself of the feeling that he was not alone on that path. The sun was completely blotted out by the black clouds, and visibility rapidly worsened.

Rain began to sheet down, slight at first, then torrential. Thunder claps were overhead, and lightning sizzled over the hill. Bryn, soaked, forced himself to run faster. His chest was aching as his mind's eye played tricks. He thought he could see a shadowy figure keeping pace with him, and tried to dismiss it as a trick of the failing light.

His concern increased as he watched his dog. Cadno, hackles raised, darted from the path to where Bryn thought he saw the figure, and barked madly.

'Come back here,' said Bryn, his voice hoarse with fear. Is there really someone, or something nearby, he thought? Must be a trick of the light, I'm imagining things.

'Anyone there?' he cried as Cadno trotted back and ran by his side. The dog would occasionally growl, as though warning an intruder to keep their distance.

Only the sound of the rain pelting down and bouncing off the ground matched the squelching of Bryn's footsteps on the muddy path.

Hair plastered over his face and clothes hanging off him in a sodden mass did not help Bryn's mounting worry. He was expecting whoever was out there in the gloom, to jump out and attack him.

As he crossed a field to the road, Bryn saw a tractor trundling along. He increased his speed, and waved his arms while he shouted. He was relieved to see the vehicle stop and wait until he climbed over a stile, followed by Cadno.

'Get in, young man, you're soaked,' said the driver, opening the door of the small cab.

'Thanks,' said Bryn, and climbed in followed by his dog. He looked back at the field and strained his eyes, trying to see who, or what, had been following them.

'Very sudden this storm,' said the driver, as he engaged gear. 'One minute bright sun, then thunder and lightning.' He grinned at Bryn's soaking clothes. 'Not to mention rain bucketing down.'

'Did you see someone chasing us?' said Bryn.

'There was only you and the dog out there,' said the driver. 'What made you ask that?'

'Must have imagined it.'

'Light plays tricks when it's fading, young man. I've seen tunnels and walls that aren't there when I've been driving in bad light.'

'You're probably right,' said Bryn, but was positive he had not imagined anything. Anyway, Cadno had seen something. He hadn't barked for nothing, and his hackles had been raised. What was happening to him in this place? Nightmares, seeing foxes that no one else could see, and now a man that was only visible to him.

'New here, aren't you?'

'Only lived here a few months. I'm Bryn Mitchell, and my mum and I live with granddad.'

'And he is?'

'Gareth Powell.'

'I know Gareth. Bit of a hard man, ex-Army I believe.'

'That's him,' said Bryn. 'He's all right most of the time, but insists on talking to mum in Welsh.' He bit his lip. 'Sorry, I didn't mean to be rude.'

The driver laughed. 'That's okay, Bryn. We're not all Welsh who live here. My name's Bob Holbrook. I'm from Cumbria, settled here some years ago. Bought a farm and married a local girl.' He turned his head to look at his companion. 'Do you play any sport?'

'Soccer's my favourite. Only seem to play rugby at my school, even though we use a soccer field. Stupid game, 'cos they never seem to know whether to run with the ball or kick it. Anyway, even the ball's a stupid shape.' Bryn reddened. 'Sorry, bet you like rugby.'

'Like to watch, but soccer's my game. Coach a youth team in town. Are you any good, Bryn?'

'Not bad.'

'How bad?'

'Was in the Rams' youth teams when we lived in Derby.'

'Really?' said Bob, interest in his voice. 'Would you like to play again?'

'Love to, but where?'

'Maybe I could arrange for you to have a trial with my lot.'

'Would you really? I miss soccer. In fact, I miss all my mates back home.'

Bob was silent as he drove, then nodded as he came to a decision. 'I'll fix a date, and pick you up myself. If you're as good as it seems you might be, then you're in.'

Bryn relaxed back in his seat. It was reassuring to find out he was not the only Englishman in Morredin, and the prospect of once again playing soccer made him grin from ear to ear. He chatted to the tractor owner until the vehicle crunched to a halt outside his grandfather's cottage.

'Thanks for the lift.'

'See you around, Bryn,' said Bob, and drove away.

Bryn enjoyed his hot bath, after his mother expressed her horror at his drowned rat appearance. Gareth merely chuckled and said that a soaking hurt no one, and it would toughen him up.

His mother had prepared a superb meal, and the room was cosy with a log fire roaring in the grate.

Bryn decided against mentioning the meeting with Selwyn, and merely talked about Idris. As he talked, his mind dwelled on the mysterious grave and the refusal of anyone to talk about the occupant. There had to be someone who, not only knew the identity, but was willing to discuss the mystery.

As he slowly chewed his food, a name crept into his subconscious. Why didn't he think of him before?

'Granddad, are you going to church tomorrow?'

'Of course, Bryn. I never miss paying my respects on the Lord's day.'

'Can I come with you?'

Gareth's fork stopped in mid air, on its way to his mouth. His eyes widened, and he carefully replaced the fork on his plate. Bryn's mother, taking a sip of water from her glass, spluttered her mouthful down herself.

'Well, can I?'

'God's house is open to everyone, Bryn.' Gareth sighed and glared at his daughter. 'But I doubt if you have had a sudden surge of religious fervour. I think there is another reason for your request.'

'There's no need to look at me like that, father,' said Bryn's mother. 'Some of us have to be on duty, Lord's day or not.'

'What's your Minister like?' said Bryn

'Very intelligent man, and writes wonderful, inspiring sermons.' Gareth wagged a finger at his grandson. 'He has an MA'

'Good,' said Bryn.

CHAPTER SEVEN

Bryn watched Anwen Hughes slowly mount the steps to the pulpit. She adjusted her spectacles, coughed twice to clear her throat, then swept the congregation with a glance that demanded immediate attention.

He had found the morning boring, the only redeeming part being the service conducted mostly in English. His grandfather had told him, as they walked to the church, that Morredin, like most Welsh churches, had been 'disestablished' in 1923.

'That means that although the services are like the English churches, we do not owe allegiance to the Queen,' said his grandfather, then hastily added, 'The church I mean.'

As they found places in the rapidly filling pews, Bryn noticed many of his school mates in attendance, including Carys and Gwyn. She had looked stunned, passing him with her parents. There seemed to be one person missing from the teaching staff, Hugh Price.

Now the atmosphere in the church crackled, and Bryn stared at his teacher. He gripped the back of the pew in front of him, as his stomach rumbled with rising panic.

This is crazy, he thought. Why should I be suddenly nervous? It's only an old church, even though it does smell stuffy, and looks a bit gloomy despite those coloured windows. Surprised to see Miss Hughes about to give a lesson. Bet she thinks she's still in school.

'Today's readings are taken from the Book of Revelation,' said Anwen, and opened the bible on the lectern. A sigh of expectation rolled over the people, as she glanced at the bible, then began speaking. She never looked at the pages again.

'From Revelation Five.' 'Then I saw in the right hand of him who sat on the throne, a scroll with writing on both sides and sealed with seven seals...'

Bryn jerked upright at what he had heard. What was it in the sentence that hit him like a bullet? 'Throne,' scroll,' seven seals.' Why did his heart suddenly thump?

"I wept and wept because no one was found who was worthy to open the scroll or look inside,"' continued Anwen. Her eyes were closed, and she swayed slightly. Head uplifted, her voice was powerful and had the rapt attention of her listeners.

Bryn's skin tingled, as he looked round at the congregation. The silence in the church was crushing. All eyes were focussed on the tiny figure in the pulpit. Anwen could have been the vicar, not the Reverend Broderick Lloyd. He was leaning forwards in his seat, listening to every word in silent concentration.

'Revelation Six,' said Anwen, and the congregation sighed with expectancy. Many mouthed the words, silently following the teacher as she continued.

They all know this, thought Bryn. Bet they can all say it from memory. What a weird lot they are, learning this rubbish. No wonder mum doesn't go to church. They want to get real in Morredin.

He felt the mounting excitement of the people as Miss Hughes continued her reading from memory, and shivered when she recounted the fourth seal.

"I heard the voice of the fourth living creature say, 'Come!' I looked and there before me was a pale horse. Its rider was named Death, and Hades was following close behind him..."

'Why is she talking about death, Granddad?' whispered Bryn, tugging his sleeve.

'Quiet, Bryn, just listen'

'Don't like it.'

'You're meant to learn from the bible lesson, not be entertained.'

Bryn blushed as nearby congregants glared in his direction, put fingers to lips, and shook their heads. He leaned forwards and bent his back, staring at his shoes.

" For the great day of their wrath has come, and who can stand." Anwen opened her eyes, and a smile slowly lit her face. She closed the bible, and looked at her rapt audience for a moment.

'Here endeth the lesson,' she said and descended the steps. Turning to the altar, she bowed, then walked to her place in the front pews.

'Wonderful,' said Bryn's grandfather.

'Awful,' mumbled Bryn, convinced that he had just been to his first and last service at Morredin's church.

Broderick Lloyd left his seat and walked in front of the pews and stopped. His thick head of grey hair, dark eyes, and lined face, was in contrast to his white cassock. He bowed to the altar then turned to smile at his congregation, nodding to Anwen.

As he looked to the back of the church, his smile vanished. Raising an arm, he pointed to the person who had quietly entered and stood near the font.

'You are not welcome here,' said the vicar, his voice quivering with emotion.

'Is this not God's house?' said Selwyn, spreading his arms.

'And are we not all God's children?'

Two men moved from their places in the back pews and moved towards him. Selwyn gripped his staff tightly, and his ferocious glare warned that physical restraint would not be tolerated. His would-be ejectors moved aside and looked to the vicar for guidance.

Broderick Lloyd glared at Selwyn for a few seconds, then quietly said, 'Let him stay. But he is here under sufferance.'

The congregation murmured their agreement, and Bryn turned round and grinned at Selwyn. He gave a thumbs-up salute, and was answered with a beaming smile from the old man, who moved and sat in the empty back pew.

Bryn followed his grandfather as they shuffled out of the church. The service had continued with increasing boredom for him. His fidgeting had resulted in whispered admonishment from his grandfather, and murmured annoyance from worshippers nearby.

'Wasn't Miss Hughes wonderful?' said Carys as she passed Bryn. Her eyes were still shining with excitement.

'I thought she was weird, getting into such a state over crazy words.' Bryn watched her walk ahead with her parents. 'Anyway, I didn't like her reading about "Death," and "Hades," whatever that is. You'll not get me here again.' He felt the glare of his grandfather and looked up. 'I mean it, Granddad, I don't want to come again.'

Gareth Powell was silent as he took his place in the queue to talk to the vicar, with Bryn by his side.

'So this is Bryn,' smiled the vicar, and shook hands. 'I do hope we'll see you regularly from now on.'

Bryn forced a smile and mumbled, 'Mebbe,' then asked,

'Can you tell me who is buried in that grave on the far side of the church?'

'Someone who was important a long time ago.'

'But who was he? He must have a name.'

'I would love to talk about it, Bryn, but as you can see, a lot of people still want to talk to me.'

'Come on,' said Gareth pushing his grandson in the back. 'If you want to ask the vicar more questions, why not arrange to go round to the vicarage?'

Bryn glanced to his left as they walked down the path. Selwyn was half-hidden behind the church, and waving to him.

Seeing that his grandfather had walked ahead, and was in earnest conversation with two men, Bryn slipped away. He picked his way across the graveyard to the back of the church.

Selwyn beamed at him. 'As you can see, my presence in this church is not exactly welcome. I know too much for their comfort.'

'Why did you come?'

'I saw you enter, so thought I'd follow,' chuckled Selwyn, and glanced across to the far side of the church grounds. 'Would I be correct in thinking that you asked Broderick Lloyd who lies in that grave over there?'

'How the h—'

'Now then, Bryn. You must not utter such words here,' Selwyn raised an eyebrow. 'Or, for that matter, anywhere.'

'You've not been to Derby,' said Bryn. 'If you thought that was bad, you should have heard some of my mates. Yes, thats was the question I was asking.'

'And what answer did you get?'

'Said he was busy and to ask him another time.'

'But you would still like to know?'

'Course. No one wants to talk about it. Even Carys wouldn't

say anything.'

Selwyn leaned on his staff and was silent. He began striding across the churchyard, having come to a decision. 'Come with me, Bryn, and let us solve the mystery of the grave that does not belong here, yet is such an important part of Morredin.'

Bryn followed the old man across the ground, whilst trying to make sense of his last words.

As he neared the distant grave, Bryn was surprised at what he saw. Expecting to see an overgrown area, only marked as a grave by the headstone, he gazed at the opposite view.

The grave was edged with a narrow bronze rail, and the grass, both on the grave and its surrounds, neatly cut. Several vases of freshly cut flowers were sitting in the centre of the grave, but it was the headstone that amazed Bryn.

The heavy slate stone was clean, and the letters had been re-carved, so the words were legible after over one and half centuries.

Bryn knelt down, and placed a hand on the slate, tracing the letters. He turned to Selwyn. 'Why is this in English, and all the other old gravestones I saw here are in Welsh?'

'That man was someone formidable here. Someone with a great deal of power.' Selwyn waved his staff round. 'You see, it was quite common in those times for anyone of importance to have their headstones in English. The ordinary people such as the farm workers, those who worked in the slate mines, and other poor people, would be remembered in their native tongue.'

'So who was he?'

'Read for yourself, Bryn.'

Bryn began to read aloud, the inscription:

'In Memory of Emrys Morgan.
Dyn Hysbys
Born 7 December 1787
Died 7 December 1840

Aged 53 years.'

He stared at the grey slate and the hairs on the back of his neck rose like the hackles of an angry dog. He turned round and looked up at Selwyn.

'What does "Din Hibis"', mean?'

'It actually says, 'Deen Husbes,' chuckled Selwyn. 'But you did quite well. Ours is not the easiest of languages to speak. As for its meaning, the simplest words are "Wise Man."'

'And was he?'

'Oh yes, young Bryn. Not only wise, but very powerful as I said before. In fact…' Selwyn stopped in mid-sentence. 'I have said enough for now, I think.' He turned on his heel and strode quickly across the grass. 'Come, Bryn. Your grandfather will think I've abducted you.'

Bryn glanced back at the grave as he trotted after Selwyn. It was obvious the old man did not want to talk further about the mysterious man in the grave.

'Odd, that, on the headstone,' said Bryn

'And what would that be?'

'Well, he was born and died on 7 December. Bet there's not many people that happens to.'

'Very perceptive. But then, as I said, the man who lies in that grave was someone very special.' Selwyn's voice was grim as he added, 'And that is why the number "seven"' is special in these parts.'

Bryn walked in silence, thinking about what Selwyn had said, and cast his mind back to the sermon. He now realised why the beginning of Miss Hughes' reading upset him. It was the reference to 'seven seals'. But he hadn't heard of Emrys Morgan then, nor the significance of the number.

Anyway, I've also a secret which I think I'll keep to myself, thought Bryn. It can wait until I find out more about Emrys Morgan.

Selwyn left him as they passed under the lychgate,

and Bryn ran along the road in the direction of home. His grandfather was already inside when he entered.

'Where did you get to?'

'Just wandered round the churchyard, and…'

'Don't lie to me, young man,' said Gareth, his voice quivering with anger.

'I'm not lying.'

'I saw you walking off with, him.'

'You mean Selwyn,' said Bryn, annoyed that he had been spotted.

'Yes, Selwyn. That man I told you not to see. A man who, as you saw for yourself, desecrates the house of God.'

'Desi what?'

Gareth sighed and shook his head. 'Let us just say that he is an intruder in our church. He is not wanted'

"cos he knows too much?'

'What makes you say that?' said Gareth, his voice hard.

'He told me,' said Bryn, seeing a flicker of anxiety in his grandfather's eyes. 'In fact he said a lot when we walked to that grave on its own.'

'And just what nonsense did he tell you?'

'Said the man in the grave was an important person.'

'That much is true.' Gareth tried to sound casual as he asked, 'And what else did he tell you?'

'That's the funny thing. He said it could wait. So who was this Emrys Morgan, Granddad?'

Gareth filled the kettle with water and lit a gas ring on the cooker. He was silent as the kettle was placed on the ring.

'Like Selwyn, I do not think you need to know everything about Emrys Morgan. He was a very important man in his time. Owned much of the land and farms round here, and was well respected.'

'Don't understand why he's not buried with everyone else. If he was such an important man, I'd have thought he'd be right in the middle, with the biggest stone on his grave.'

Bryn walked across to a cupboard and took out two mugs. Taking them to his grandfather, he touched his arm, and when Gareth looked at him, said, 'So why is he away from everyone else, Granddad?'

'There are some things you do not need not know, Bryn, and this is one of them.' Gareth put two tea bags in a teapot and watched steam begin to rise from the kettle.

'Why not?'

'I do not have to explain myself to you, Bryn. I have said my final word on the subject. Now go to your room and get out of those tidy clothes if you are going to play with Cadno. I'll make some sandwiches for our lunch. We'll be having roast beef for supper, when your mother comes home.'

Bryn began to climb the stairs, then stopped, turned round and called, 'Granddad?'

'What is it now?'

'Just one question.'

'And?'

'I suppose Emrys is a Welsh name.'

'Yes.'

'What does it mean?'

'Immortal.'

Bryn wondered what that meant but decided not to ask. He had noticed his grandfather's hand tremble as he poured the hot water into the teapot. This mysterious man from years ago still had power in the village, but why?

CHAPTER EIGHT

Cadno bounded along the field, barking happily at the birds, the sky and the world. He was a happy dog now Bryn had taken him for a walk after lunch. His young master shuffled through the rough grass, deep in thought.

Lunch with grandfather had been eaten silently. Afterwards, Bryn had gone to his room, taken a biro and after a few moments contemplation began writing in a small notebook.

'<u>What Do I Know</u>.

1. I have nightmares, not so many recently.

2. I see foxes, but nobody else does. Why only me, am I going potty. And another thing, why does everyone look almost scared when I talk about it.

3. Selwyn. No one likes him, except me. Why? He knows a lot about this place but won't tell me. And why did the vicar say he wasn't welcome in church. Funny lot, 'cos I thought everyone was welcome in church. This gets crazier.

4. This is the best bit. Who is this Emrys Morgan, and why is his grave away from the others? There's a story there, a mystery for Detective Bryn Mitchell to sort out.

5. Carys and Gwyn seem friends, but there's something going on, and I don't mean 'cos they keep talking to each

other in Welsh.

6. There's something special about number 'seven'.

<u>What Must I Find Out</u>

1.What has Selwyn done to upset everyone, including granddad. Or does he know something, awful about this place, and they are all frightened of him?

2. Are foxes important, and if not, why do I see them?

3. Emrys Morgan. Now that is a mystery. Must find out more about him, but where do I start?

4. Miss Hughes and that Revelation thing. Was it when she talked about 'seven' that upset me. Must see if there's more to read.

5. Carys and the others. Have they got a secret club? Another mystery for Detective Bryn Mitchell.

6. Who is still putting flowers on that grave.'

Bryn tapped his teeth with the end of the pen and read his words carefully. He stroked Cadno's head when the dog pushed open the door to sit by his side.

'Know what, Cadno?' said Bryn. 'There's a lot of funny things going on here. Trouble is no one wants to talk about it. Wish the gang were here, especially Rod, his dad being a copper.'

He made one more entry before closing his notebook and hiding it under the mattress. It was his secret, to refer to when needed. Calling Cadno, he left his room, and the cottage without saying anything to his grandfather.

The sky was overcast, and Bryn was glad he had taken his anorak as he was sure it would rain later. He could see the twin peaks of the Court of Foxes, stabbing the darkening clouds. That hill had secrets, but no one was prepared to talk. Was it something to do with the strange Emrys Morgan, or maybe the story of the foxes meeting with their king?

'That's a load of rubbish for a start,' said Bryn to Cadno,

who had found a thick stick and brought it back. 'A fox king, Cadno. Whatever will they think of next, Vampires living here?' Bryn laughed, but looked furtively round just in case he was being followed. Shadows in the hollows on the hillside could take any shape with a fertile imagination.

He threw the stick for his dog, and saw it land in a bush. A crow hurtled skywards with a squawk of annoyance, and Cadno threw himself in the air to try and catch the bird.

'Thinks he's a cat, does he?'

Bryn turned round to see the amused face of Idris as he trotted towards him, dressed in a grey tracksuit and trainers.

'Been watching you for some time,' said Idris. 'I usually go for a run along here at weekends.' He slowed down to walking pace.

'Training for something?'

'Nothing special, see. Just like to keep fit, though I do play rugby and football. So what are you doing out here, talking to yourself.'

'You heard then,' said Bryn, and continued walking. He was uncomfortable with the tall, athletic Idris by his side. He remembered their first encounter and the hostility.

'I heard,' said Idris. 'You weren't whispering.'

'Just thinking aloud, that's all.'

'And what was so important to make you think aloud,' said Idris, deliberately saying the last two words slowly.

'What do you know about a fox king, that hill over there, and the mysterious Emrys Morgan?'

Idris walked in silence, picking up the stick, which Cadno had deposited at his feet, and throwing it.

'Well?'

'There are lots of stories in these parts, see, going back hundreds of years, and…'

'But these aren't just stories, are they? Emrys Morgan is real enough. I've seen his grave. Not that it helps much, 'cos, apart from someone putting flowers on his grave, I don't know much about him, except when he was born and died.'

'Emrys Morgan was a wizard, so it is said round here,' said Idris, after a moment's silence.

'Do you believe that? I mean do you really think he could cast spells and make magic?'

'I believe he was a very clever and wise man.'

'You've not answered my question.'

Idris began jogging again, and Bryn tried to keep pace with him. Cadno, thinking this a new game, ran round them, and barked enthusiastically.

'I think it's going to rain, so will leave you now and finish my run,' said Idris, and quickened his pace. Bryn, determined to learn more, matched his speed.

'You're a good runner, but you'll not keep up for long.'

'We'll see,' said Bryn, and settled into a steady rhythm by his side. He's not to know that I trained hard with my team back home in Derby. And when I was training with the Rams' youth teams that was real hard. They made us train 'till it hurt. Bet Idris doesn't know what real 'hurt' is.

They covered the ground quickly, following the curves of the stream. Bryn was in new territory, never having walked so far from home. He followed Idris past the stepping stones until they had left the village behind.

Idris flashed him a smile and, turning off the path, began climbing upwards, breathing deeply.

They were passing through clumps of gorse, the ground very uneven, with dangerous hollows waiting to twist an ankle or send a runner sprawling.

Idris pointed to a winding track that led upwards, and slowed to a gentle trot.

'If you want to find out more, follow that track up to the top of the first hill,' he said, then before Bryn could react, sprinted away to disappear over the brow of a hillock.

'What will I find?' cried Bryn, but only the birds answered, and he shivered as a cold gust tumbled down the hill.

He looked up to see the thickening white clouds rapidly becoming black in the centre.

'Yeah, he's right. It's going to rain later. Suppose we'd better head back.'

Bryn turned back along the path then glanced at the track, which meandered up the hill. Shouldn't take long to get to the top, and Idris had said I'd find something interesting.

A warning voice told him that maybe Idris was fooling, having fun at his expense. There wasn't anything interesting to find. Bryn called Cadno, and stepped off the path to the track.

As he climbed, Bryn could see the grass become sparse, and covered with clusters of dark green bushes. Trees rose on either side of the track, herded together, their tops swaying in unison with the increasing wind.

He stopped and looked back, wiping a hand across his sweating brow. The anorak was hot to wear, and he was surprised to see how far he had climbed.

'Looks a long way down, Cadno,' he said to his dog which had trotted back and sat down, waiting patiently. 'Still, I can just see the top of the hill, so not much further to go.'

He plodded on, having increasing doubts about his decision to continue, seeing the sky had become increasingly darker. Droplets of rain splashing on his head did not help his discomfort. If there were nothing to be seen, then it would be a long walk home, and the chances of a soaking and the anger of mum.

A fine mist of rain obscured the view as he stood on the top and looked down the other side. The track ended at the summit of the hill.

'Can't see anything, Cadno,' said Bryn, wiping the rain

from his eyes. 'Not that I know what I'm supposed to see. What a ruddy idiot I am, believing Idris. Bet he's laughing his head off, and can't wait to tell the others.'

He scanned the rolling ground below. Roughly a hundred metres from the top, the steep side of the hill flattened into a rough field, then climbed upwards again to another, smaller, hillock. Outcrops of rock, grey and jagged, protruded from the grass.

Looking to his left, Bryn could see a dark hollow where the field joined the base of the hillock. Surrounded by bushes, it looked gloomy and menacing.

Slipping and sliding down the slope, he jogged across the field to the hollow. Sudden panic swept over him. He wanted to turn round and go home, but curiosity forced him on.

'It's so dark over there,' said Bryn to Cadno. 'Why don't I just pack up before we're both soaked?'

He already knew the answer, and was heading towards the place Idris told him. What was waiting? Something exciting, or, frightening?

Bryn stopped when he reached the edge of a sudden drop from the field to tumbled rocks. As he clambered down the rocks, he could see what looked like a cleft in the rock face at the base of the hollow.

Obscured by a tangled undergrowth of gorse bushes, and trees growing out of the ground and rocks, was a dark entrance. Bryn stopped and stared with a sharp intake of breath. He was facing the entrance to a cave, but how far and how deep did it penetrate the hillock?

'There's only one way to find out, Cadno, and that's to go in.'

Cadno growled at the entrance, his hackles erect. He sensed something wrong in the depths of the cave, and would not move.

'That settles it,' said Bryn as the misty rain turned to a

sudden downpour as a squall passed overhead. The noise of the rain hammering down echoed inside the cave as they pushed the thin trees aside to enter. The atmosphere was chilly, and the rocks glistened with damp.

Bryn's eyes gradually adjusted to the darkness, and he tingled at the sight. This was not an empty cave, but was being used for some purpose. To his right, on a rocky outcrop, was a half-used candle stuck on an old cracked saucer, which also held a box of matches.

The match rasped as it was struck, and flickered into flame, shadows appearing on the cave walls. Bryn cupped the match until it had a steady glow, then lit the candle.

He held up the saucer, and the yellow light flickered in a draft, making the many shadows dance madly. This was not a place for the faint-hearted or those with a vivid imagination.

He shuffled across the stone strewn floor, weaving the candle from side to side. Reaching out to touch the rocky wall to steady himself as he stumbled, he shivered. The rock was icy cold.

'What is this place?' said Bryn aloud. 'More to the point, who comes here?'

Cadno stayed by the entrance, barking madly at his young master to leave. With a final whimper, the dog lay down and placed his face between his paws, watching.

Bryn saw partially used candles stuck on rocky ledges, and recoiled in alarm when he spied two, much larger candles on either side of a slab of stone

The slab had been lifted on top of two other stones so that it resembled a table.

'Or an altar,' whispered Bryn, staring at the two candles on either side. His concern increased as he observed their colour. They were black.

'What happens here?' Bryn looked round, expecting something to leap out. Yet he stayed, not knowing why, only knowing he had to.

Cadno whined, but Bryn ignored the pleas of his dog to leave, and touched the melted wax on the slab. It was in rivulets, snaking over the stone and dropping from the edge to a large, solid pool on the floor. Whoever came here, was a frequent visitor.

Bryn knelt down and eased his candle to floor level so that he could look under the slab. A small, well-used wooden box lay on the stones.

A tingle of anticipation and fear caressed his skin as he eased out the box. It was very old, and rough to the touch. Made of a dark wood, the lid had brass hinges. A heavy-looking metal clasp closed the lid, and was secured by a large modern padlock.

'Damn!' mouthed Bryn, and moved his candle around the space under the slab. 'There's got be a key somewhere.'

Cadno barked and Bryn turned round, ordering, 'Quiet. Just have patience.'

His fingers scrabbled in the stones and earth. Something tickled the back of one hand. Bryn yelled, and shook his hand vigorously to dislodge a large spider, which ran across the ground and up the wall.

Giving himself a few moments to recover, Bryn sat on the ground. Clasping his hands round his bent legs, he looked round the cave. The candle was burning well. Too well, thought Bryn. There's not much time left. Must find that key. Can't be far away, it's not a big cave.

He noticed a tiny cleft in the rock just above the slab, and he stood up then leaned over the slab, which he was now convinced served as an altar.

The candle was raised so that its light shone in the cleft. Something glinted in the glow.

'Yes,' whispered Bryn, and reached inside to extract a key. He sat down, and pulled the box towards him. The lock was stiff, and Bryn struggled to turn the key, but eventually there was a click as the padlock opened.

The candlelight was flickering as it neared the end of its life, and he knew he had to work fast.

Trembling hands opened the lid, and he stared at the contents of the box. There was just one book inside. It was small, thick, and bound with old, heavily creased leather. A book that had been often used. A book, so important, it had to be kept under lock and key.

The candle was now flickering violently, warning of imminent darkness. Bryn opened the book and looked at handwritten words that were alien to him. The writing was neat and the ink fading. This book had been written many years ago. He read what seemed to be prayers, and he stared at one sentence then whispered the words.

'Let the power come soon so that the fiery red horse and its rider will wreak havoc on earth and men will slay each other.' He felt compelled to read more, but the flickering candle was telling him time was short.

Reluctantly, he closed the book, and locked the box, replacing it under the stone slab. The key was back in the rocky cleft, and he walked out of the cave, leaving the spent candle in its saucer where he had found it.

Cadno wagged his tail, happy they were leaving. The rain had gone, leaving water dripping from the trees over the entrance, making the rocks slippery.

Bryn looked back at the cave, and carefully climbed over the rocky ground until they were back in the field. The ground was turning to mud with the downpour, and his trainers were soon covered in a sticky brown mess.

As he began the treck home, he turned round and frowned. Someone was standing at the top of the far hillock staring at him. Before he had time to recognise the observer, the figure had disappeared.

'Wonder if he goes to that cave?' Bryn asked Cadno, who barked in reply and ran ahead. 'If he does, he'll soon realise I've been inside.'

As he jogged along the track by the stream, Bryn had another thought. He had been calling the person on top of the hill, 'he.' Supposing it was a 'she,' possibly Carys?

There was definitely something weird going on in that cave. Maybe there was a secret society meeting there, but for what purpose? Selwyn had said there were strange things in Morredin, and the writing in that old book was certainly very odd.

As he opened the gate to his grandfather's cottage, he saw his mother. She was standing in the cottage doorway, arms folded. Her grim face made it obvious to Bryn that she was not pleased to see him.

'Where have you been all this time?'

'Out,' said Bryn, trying to push past.

'I know that, young man. Your grandfather's been worried sick.'

'He knew I was taking Cadno out for a walk,'

'You've been gone for hours,' said his mother, her eyes glinting. 'Didn't think of telling him you'd be gone so long, did you?'

Bryn shrugged his shoulders. 'Didn't know I would be, did I?'

'That's no answer, and you know it.'

'Know what, Mum?' said Bryn, tiredness reducing his patience. 'You sound just like the way you talked to dad.'

He pushed past, pulled off his trainers, and threw them on the floor inside the doorway. Before his mother could reply, he ran up the stairs to his room, ignoring the stern glare from his grandfather.

'Bryn!' screamed his mother. 'Come down here this minute.'

He heard her talk to his grandfather, and guessed from the heated voices, that he was the subject of discussion.

What a pain grownups are. Always asking questions. Always wanting to know what you've done and where you've been. I never ask Mum or Granddad what they're up to. That's different.

Bryn reached an arm under his mattress and pulled out his notebook. He lay on his back on the bed and read his previous notes. It was time to write down his latest thoughts.

He could hear his mother crying downstairs, and knew that he would apologise for upsetting her. Anything to keep the peace, and stopping Granddad from blowing his cool again.

Right, he thought, now let's make some notes on that cave. There's only really one thing that's struck me about it.

He picked up his biro and wrote a few sentences about meeting Idris, the cave, and it being used for some purpose. 'Does Idris go to the meetings, whatever they are?' Bryn then ended his notes by writing: 'It's a weird cave, and a bit frightening. But it's nothing like the cave in my dreams. Does that cave really exist and where is it?' He chewed the end of the biro, then added his final comment: 'I think my cave is real, and it's round here somewhere.'

CHAPTER NINE

Bryn walked through the school gates, his mind on the cold atmosphere he had left behind. Supper the previous night had been eaten in silence. He had meant to apologise to his mother, but his grandfather had killed that idea.

'If you were my son, I'd thrash you for speaking to your mother like that,' he said as Bryn descended the stairs. 'You're an ungrateful boy.'

'Then I'm lucky you're not, aren't I, Granddad? And Dad never hit me anyway.'

He had watched his grandfather redden with anger, open and close his mouth, not knowing how to respond. He stormed out of the room. Bryn, once again, wished he could turn back the clock and transport himself and his mother back to Derby.

He felt a wet nose pushed into his hand, and looked down.

Cadno was sitting by his side, sensing something was wrong.

'I wouldn't go back without you,' said Bryn. 'You're about the only friend I can rely on in this place. Granddad thinks he's still in the Army. Mum's happy one minute and fed up the next.' He walked to the door and called to his dog to follow. 'Come on, let's go out and have a game. Maybe they'll have cooled down a bit when we come back.'

He thought about the rest of that Sunday as he wandered into the playground.

Supper had been a nightmare of silence. No one wanted to speak, and his mother had served himself and his grandfather, then announced she was not hungry, and left the room.

Bryn ate his food quickly, eyes fixed on his plate. He did not want to see the hostile, angry face of his grandfather. The rest of the evening had been spent mostly in his room, reading and thinking.

As an afterthought, he quickly did the homework set by Hugh Price. His mind was on other things with the result that he began writing without much thought. He read a few lines, then ripped the page out of his exercise book and began again.

Have a good weekend?' said Gwyn.

'Had a row with Mum and Granddad, over nothing. No one spoke to each other all Sunday. Well, most of it anyway.' Bryn forced a laugh. 'Yeah, you could say it was different, but not enjoyable.'

'Didn't you go out then?'

'Nowhere special,' said Bryn. 'There isn't anywhere special to see round here, is there?'

'What do you mean by 'special'?'

'I dunno, perhaps somewhere where no one else knows about it.'

Gwyn stared at Bryn. 'What sort of place?'

'You tell me. I've only just come here.'

They walked in silence for a few steps, then Gwyn shook his head. 'Well I can't think of anywhere that special, see. There's the gold mines at Twyn, but then lots of visitors come to see them.'

Bryn looked at his companion and thought that he did not sound convincing. He was sure Gwyn knew about that cave. Maybe he had been inside, and taken part in some weirdo stunt. Oh, yes, Gwyn knew much more than he was saying.

He saw Carys walk towards them, then pass without saying a word and run to a group of girls.

'What's wrong with her?'

'Not sure,' said Gwyn. 'I'll find out.' He ran to join her.

Bryn entered the school, passing Miss Hughes. She smiled and told him how pleased she was to see him at church.

'Your grandfather is a fine man, Bryn. You could do worse than follow his example, and come to church every Sunday from now on.'

'Yes, Miss Hughes,' said Bryn, then stopped and walked back. 'Do you know everything from memory in that book you used?'

'No, Bryn, why?' She allowed a brief smile to cross her face. 'And by the way, that "book" is the Bible.'

'Just that you never looked at it once, and I noticed most in church seemed to know the words as well.'

His teacher took off her glasses and held them up to the light as if looking for dust. 'It's a lovely old church, going back a long time, and the vicar is a fine man.'

She turned to greet some more pupils. Bryn, wondering why Miss Hughes had changed the subject, entered the school. Why didn't she want to talk about the Revelation thing, he thought as he walked to the cloakroom.

'Penny for them,' said Carys behind him.

'Talking to me, are you?'

'Of course. Why shouldn't I?'

"cos you walked past me out there without saying a word.'

'Sorry, Bryn. Had a lot on my mind.' She placed her jacket on a peg, then turned round, smiling. 'Heard you had an interesting weekend.'

'Not really, just rows at home.' Bryn slowly took off his anorak, and tried to sound casual.

'Gwyn must have been wrong then. He's not very bright at the best of times.'

Bryn looked into the innocent eyes of Carys and thought this was like a cat stalking a mouse. She thinks that I have been somewhere interesting, but is not certain, and hopes to get more from me. Fat chance she's got. But then again, maybe she wasn't the person I saw staring at me on Sunday. Maybe she doesn't know about the hidden cave. But then, maybe she does and wonders if I found it.

'I went to see that grave on its own, after the service was over.' Bryn picked up his backpack and followed Carys out of the cloakroom. 'Surprised to see someone still looks after it after all that time.' He glanced at Carys but she merely smiled and waved to some friends.

'Don't you think that's odd?'

'Not really, why should I?'

'Well, back in Derby, I never saw really old graves looked after like this one. Anyway, there's lots of old graves with headstones almost down. And the writing's gone on most, but someone thinks a lot of this Emrys Morgan.' Bryn touched her arm. 'So who was he, Carys?'

'Lots of stories about him, and…'

'Dyn Hysbys.'

'The wise man,' whispered Carys.

'So you do know about him.'

'You weren't born here, Bryn, so don't ask anymore. Just

forget about it.' Carys bit her lip, then looked at him. 'Emrys was someone who is still remembered with respect and...'

'Fear?' said Bryn looking at her trembling mouth. She rushed away to join another group of children.

As he walked along the corridor to his classroom, after assembly in the small hall, Bryn shivered as he sensed a presence behind him. He turned his head, and had a glimpse, or thought he had, of a shadowy figure walking among the pupils.

Was it a ghost walking though the school? Who was it, and why hadn't he heard about it before? And why was it only him who saw the figure? The other children were seemingly unaware of the spectre walking with them.

Entering the classroom he was shocked to realise that it was the same feeling he felt when coming home from his walk with Cadno. The same fear, and the same, person. Yes, Bryn thought, that vague shadowy image was a person. He had no idea if it was a man or woman, or child even, but was sure it was human.

Must be a ghost, but who? And why should he see it? After all, Carys was correct. He didn't belong here, even though mum and granddad were born in Morredin.

'This place is getting to me,' said Bryn quietly, as he walked to his desk. He opened his bag and took out his books.

'Talking to yourself again I see,' said Carys.

'Just thinking aloud,' Bryn turned round and stared at her mocking eyes. 'You said something about me not belonging here. Is it "cos I'm not Welsh?'

'Forget it, Bryn, it's not important.'

'Well you thought it was a few minutes ago. Practically snapped my head off.'

'Didn't mean to, but...'

'Found a cave,' said Bryn, deciding to test her reaction. He saw, with satisfaction, her face pale.

'Where?'

'Not sure, somewhere in the hills.'

'How?'

'Out walking with Cadno,' said Bryn, not knowing why he did not include Idris in his reply.

'There's loads of caves round here, Bryn. I can take you to one just a short walk from the school.'

'Not this one,' said Bryn, then turned his back on her as Hugh Price entered the classroom and coughed for attention.

Bryn saw Carys give him a backwards glance then go to her desk. He found it very satisfying to see the concern in her eyes.

Bet she tries to find out more, he thought. I've got her rattled. Maybe she thinks I don't belong here, but I am here, though I just wish we could go back to my mates in Derby, and yell out, 'Come on the Rams' on Saturdays.

'I trust you have all done the homework I set for the weekend?' The teacher's voice was more challenging than questioning. 'It was simple enough, just a short description of the most exciting event you experienced last weekend.'

He scanned his class and noted that most heads nodded. He looked down at his notes then stared at Bryn. 'What about you, Bryn? Why not read us your epistle, and show us how well you can write.'

An excited restlessness swept through the classroom as Bryn opened his exercise book. Even the release of pressure by Hugh Price in his customary manner could not disturb the tension.

Bryn wondered why he had been selected to go first. Unless, he looked up quickly as he scanned his homework. Unless the watcher on the hill had been Mr Price, and he is curious to find out what I've written. But then why should the whole class be, almost excited, to hear me?

'When you are ready, Bryn.'

'Yes, sir,' said Bryn. 'It's written in English.'

'Why doesn't that surprise me?' said Hugh as the classroom giggled until silenced by his glare. 'Begin then. Electrify us with your literary expertise, and your enjoyment of the English language. Let the power of your prose flow over us like a tidal wave. Enthral us with the excitement of your adventures.' He sat down in the chair behind his desk and leaned back. He closed his eyes, turned his head towards the ceiling and folded his arms as he said, 'Commence.'

Bryn was aware of the increasing tension in the room. He wondered what they were expecting to hear. He stared at the page, and smiled. This was not the story he had first written concerning the weekend. On reflection, he had ripped out that version.

'Last Sunday I went with my grandfather to church. It is a very old church, and has some stained glass windows. The vicar is an okay guy I guess, and seemed quite friendly. The seats are very hard and someone has used a penknife to scratch at the back of the seat in front of me. I was surprised to see Miss Hughes give the lesson and even more surprised when she hardly looked at the book. She seemed to know every word. So did the people in church. The lesson was from the Book of Revelation and was all about awful things. I don't know why she chose such an unhappy story as there are more fun stories she could have used. After the service was over I went to see a grave which was at the other end of the church grounds.' Bryn glanced at his teacher, who opened his eyes and looked at him.

'Is that it?'

'Didn't know how long you wanted me to read, sir.'

'And was this grave interesting? Did you find out much about the occupant?'

'Yes, sir. Emrys Morgan is buried there, and the funny thing is he was born and died on the same date in December.'

'Was that the only thing of interest you did last weekend?' said Hugh Price, suddenly very interested in the tips of his fingers.'I wouldn't have thought going to church and seeing a grave was the epitome of excitement. Even if you were entertained by Miss Hughes.'

Bryn glanced at his exercise book, excited. He was sure Mr Price had been expecting another story. The story he had ripped out.

He shook his head. 'No, sir, that's about it, but I have a question. What does "epitome"' mean?'

'It means "high quality", Bryn,' said the teacher, and a smile lit his eyes. 'And I have a question for you. What does 'okay guy' mean?'

Bryn shrugged his shoulders.'An 'okay guy' is… is someone who's okay, sir.'

'I'm sure there's not a Welsh translation, though I will find out,' said the teacher. 'Thank you, Bryn. We have all been enthralled by your adventures. I do hope that by the time you leave my administration, your standard of writing will have markedly improved.'

Bryn pushed open the gate and ambled down the short path to the cottage. He had walked home after school on his own. He had been thinking all day about that first lesson. Carys and Gwyn had tried to be friendly and talk about the weekend. Bryn guessed they knew he had done something far more exciting than just going to church and visiting Emrys Morgan's grave.

He had forgotten about the bad atmosphere he had left behind at home. Now he had to face an angry grandfather and try and make peace before his mother returned.

'Have a good day at school, Bryn?' said Gareth, sitting in his favourite armchair by the fireplace. Cadno, who had been lying by his side, sprang to his feet as Bryn opened the door.

'Had to read out my homework for Farty Hugh. Don't think he was terribly impressed with my story about going to church.' He looked round. 'Mum not home yet?'

'No, Bryn, and I want a word with you about your behaviour yesterday before she comes home.' Gareth sighed and shook his head. 'And I do wish you did not call your teacher in such a disrespectful manner.'

'What, 'Farty'? Well he does, often. The joke is I don't think he knows it's him.' Bryn slumped into a kitchen chair and stroked Cadno's head. 'Thing is, Granddad, it's this place. It's getting to me. Something odd here, and anyway, today Carys told me I didn't belong here.'

'She actually said that?'

'Not in as many words, but we were talking about something, and…'

'What?'

'Emrys Morgan. Carys then said I should forget about him as I wasn't born here. So it's the same as saying I'm not wanted here, isn't it, Granddad?' He looked at Gareth, and saw the newspaper he was holding flutter as his hand trembled.

'Morredin does have many secrets, so I believe,' said Gareth, and carefully folded the paper. He was silent for a few seconds, then continued, staring at the fireplace. 'Even as a child, I was aware there seemed to be a group who were apart from the rest of the villagers. My parents were not in that group and warned me against getting too involved with their children.' A weak smile crossed his face. 'That was not easy in those days. The village was much smaller than today, so the children had to mix with each other. But something used to happen and I was excluded.' He sat up and stared into the fireplace.

'And?' said Bryn, staring at his grandfather. Even Cadno appreciated the tension, and he quivered, ears erect.

'The group, with the children, would go out of the village and walk up the hills. It was, frightening, because they would not say a word as they left the village. It was always at night, and I remember looking out of my bedroom window and seeing a line of torches snaking up the hill…'

'Which hill?' whispered Bryn.

'Court of Foxes,' said Gareth, then smiled at his grandson. 'That was a long time ago. I joined the Army when still a boy, and only came home on leave. So many changes over the years, and I served all over the world. Met your grandma in Cyprus, when stationed out there. She was also Welsh, and her father was in the RAF As we both could speak the language, it was fun to keep it alive and have conversations.

'When we married, it was a life of married quarters until I was demobbed and we came back here. Poor love, didn't have long here until bloody cancer took her from us.'

Bryn left his chair and walked over to his grandfather. Putting his arms round the older man's shoulders, he had an overwhelming feeling of guilt.

'Sorry, Granddad. I didn't ever get to meet Grandma, did I?'

'No, Bryn, and more's the pity.'

'What about Mum? Did she know anything about what was going on here?'

'Oh, she heard rumours, but remember, her schooling was done all over the world. Best school that is, seeing life. When we came here on leave, it was a bit of a squeeze in this cottage, what with my parents living here.'

'Did your parents know of the secret?'

Gareth was silent, then stood up, and walked to the kitchen. He pulled out a bag of potatoes and began to peal them, only the splash as he threw them into a pan of water breaking the silence.

'Yes,' he said quietly, then looked up as the sound of a car halting outside the cottage broke the spell.

'It's your mother, Bryn, so better make your peace with her.' He turned round and wagged the knife. 'I don't want you discussing what we've been talking about with her. Understand?'

Bryn nodded and watched the door open and his mother enter. I might not be able to talk to Mum, but I've a lot more questions to ask Granddad.

CHAPTER TEN

B ryn struggled up the hillside, his feet sinking into the clinging, sticky mud, up to his ankles. Every footstep was an effort, his thighs and leg muscles aching. He wanted to stop for a rest, but could not. Something would not allow him.

Every time he stumbled, he heard a deep, threatening voice command him to continue. The voice surrounded him with its menace. He felt enveloped in a power that controlled him, but if he looked round there was no one on that hillside with him.

'You cannot stop now. Keep moving. Force your legs to move you onwards and upwards. There is no time for rest or delay. I have waited far too long, Bryn, for you to come.'

'I must have a rest,' he heard himself reply. 'My heart's bursting, and my chest aches. It's like having a steel band round me, getting tighter and tighter.'

As he staggered along the winding track, the hill was steeper. It seemed to become more vertical with each step, and as he climbed, a wind screeched from the summit and hurtled down. He bent his head and body to fight the gusts trying to tumble him down the hill.

The noise increased and Bryn could hear that it had become the sound of a multitude of people moaning and screaming in pain and fear. As the sky darkened, the rumble of thunder rolled round the hill like a hundred beating drums. It drowned the cries of the unseen tormented souls.

He looked upwards, and saw a white horse ride out from the clouds, followed by a fiery red one. Bryn cowered with fright, but the voice talking to him had no pity.

'No stopping, Bryn, not now. See my power, see your destiny.'

A black horse hurtled out of the clouds, as lightning sizzled and crashed in the hills. Bryn shivered with fear as he cried out, 'I want to go home. I don't want to go on.'

'But you must, you have no choice. See what I can do.'

The cries of the unseen people were hushed as though they knew something awful was to happen. The thunder died and the lightning faded. Bryn yelled out that he did not want to see, and the tears tumbled down his face. But he looked upwards.

The sky was now a fiery red, and the silence ominous. Time stood still, waiting for something awesome. Out of the deepest red cloud strode a magnificent pale horse. On its back was a figure dressed in black. A cowl covered the face, but when the horse was overhead, the cowl was thrown back.

Bryn screamed with fright as he saw a grinning skull. An

arm was raised in salute, the bones revealed as the sleeve fell back.

Flames hurtled from the red sky and reached down to earth, which instantly caught fire. The whole hillside was aflame, the crackling flames surrounding a terrified Bryn. He could hardly breathe in the intense heat. There was no escape from the wall of fire slowly moving towards him, the thunder of burning deafening.

'See my friend. He is named "Death" and will do my bidding when the time is right. You will help me. See how he rides majestically through the fire, the flames parting in supplication.'

'No! No!' cried Bryn, and slumped to the ground, covering his head in his arms as red rain began to fall. The flames died in the downpour. Heavier and heavier came the red deluge, and he could only cower and look with horror, as he was soaked in warm sticky blood, which ran down the hillside.

Bryn lay on his back staring at the bedroom ceiling. He felt drained and was aware of his thumping heart and the sweat pouring down his face.

His nightmare had returned, but this was something else, apart from not being in the cave. This one seemed to be showing a terror yet to come, which involved him.

'Bryn, love, are you alright?' said his mother, knocking on his door.

'Had a bad dream, Mum. A real bad one this time, much worse than the others.'

His mother entered his room, sat on his bed and cradled his head. She gently rocked him, stroking his hair, while murmuring, 'Shh. I'm here now.' She felt his forehead and withdrew her wet hand.

'Bryn, you're very hot and the sweat's pouring off you. I think you've caught a chill from that soaking at the weekend. No wonder you were having nightmares. Wouldn't be surprised if you have a temperature. I'll get a thermometer in a minute.'

She plumped the pillow and laid his head back. 'You are staying in bed, young man, no school for you today. I'll get you a hot drink, then phone the school when they open. Look at the time? It's only five.'

Bryn watched her walk to the door, then smile as she said, 'Try and get some sleep after you've had your drink. I wouldn't worry about that dream. Your mind plays tricks when you have a fever.'

'Yes, Mum,' said Bryn, as she closed the door behind her. He stared at the ceiling, thinking about his dream as his heartbeat returned to normal. His nightmare had nothing to do with a fever. The heat was real, and he had expected to be burnt alive any minute. The experience had been a message from someone. The only question being who, and why?

At least he was friends with Mum again. It had all ended in tears, and as they hugged each other, he had told her how much he loved her, and it was all dad's fault.

"cos if he'd been a proper dad, we'd still be in Derby. I'd have my pals, and be playing proper football.'

'He was a good dad at first, Bryn. But when he was made redundant, it hurt him very badly.'

'Lots of my pals' dads had no job.'

'I know, but your father was a very proud man, and he'd worked for that company for years. He couldn't get used to not having a job and having to collect social security each week. He felt, less of a man with me working.'

'Is that why he got drunk so often?'

'Guess so, Bryn, though that's no excuse. Neither is him taking his anger out on me and our home.' She cupped Bryn's chin and her eyes became moist. 'If he hadn't left us, I would have walked out on him. I'd had enough of his temper, and hitting me.'

'But he never hit me, did he?'

'No, Bryn. He was so proud when Derby County invited you to join their youth training. Even though he'd left us, he would tell all his pals in the pubs about you. He said he was looking forward to seeing you at Pride Park, leading the First Team out on the pitch.'

Bryn thought about that conversation they'd had the previous evening, then tried to visualise his father. He could remember him as a tall, athletic man, with a craggy face, dark round eyes that could be gentle one minute and glitter in anger the next. Thick black wavy hair came low down his forehead. There was something else, and Bryn frowned in concentration.

He was sure it was something about his father's face, but the more he concentrated, the dimmer was the vision, until it was just a blur. So much of their former life was a blur, he thought. Guess I was only about seven when he finally left. Can still remember his fights with mum though. We were happy once. What went wrong? It can't have been just because he lost his job.

'He'd have hated it here,' said Bryn to the small clock on his bedside table. He leaned down to pull his notebook from under the mattress.

He quickly read what had been written, sucked on the end of his biro and began writing.

'What do I know?

1. Granddad is still frightened of what used to happen here when he was my age.

2. There is a secret society, 'cos I found their cave. What do they do there?

3. This Emrys Morgan thing gets crazier and crazier.

He's important to what? EVERYTHING.

<u>What must I find out?</u>
1. More about Emrys Morgan.
2. More about the meetings in the cave. Might, no, MUST find out what happens. No problem for

Detective Bryn and his dog.
3. This Revelation thing is important. Will borrow granddad's bible and find out.
4. Why has my horrible dream changed?
5. What is this trip the awful voice told me I had to make?'

Bryn read through what he had written, then placed the biro inside the notebook. He quickly pushed it under his mattress as he heard his mother knock on the door.

'Drink this, after I've taken your temperature,' she said, holding a steaming mug of hot chocolate. 'It will help you relax, and get some more sleep.' She held a hand against his forehead. 'Hm, you're not as hot as before. Anyway,' she said, placing a small thermometer under his tongue. 'By the time you've had some more sleep, it'll be too late for school.'

There was a brief silence until the thermometer was taken from Bryn's mouth and scrutinised.

'Your temperature has certainly gone down, but I don't suppose you'll mind a day off school.'

'Mum, did Granddad ever talk to you about weird things here?'

'What sort of things, Bryn?'

'Not sure, but he was telling me about seeing a crowd of people going up the Court of Foxes at night. He was probably my age at the time.' He stared at her face, trying to see surprise, or fright in her eyes, but they were blank.

'I've always been aware of rumours of wizards, magic, and bad spirits in these parts. But I never saw anything as a child. Remember, when I was your age, we were living in many countries, so never spent much time here.' She placed the mug on his bedside table, kissed him on the forehead and turned to leave the room.

'Mum,' said Bryn as she reached the door.

'What now?'

'Don't tell Granddad about what we've just talked about, will you?'

'Not if you don't want me to,' she said and closed the door behind her.

Bryn thought about what she had said. Wizards, magic, and, bad spirits. He shivered, and knew it was nothing to do with catching a chill. What if there really were bad spirits in Morredin? What if they were after him, and had been chasing him that day he took Cadno for a walk? But why him?

Then he remembered something else. Selwyn told me he stayed here because he felt he was needed here. The next time I meet him, I'll ask some more questions, and won't be satisfied until I get proper answers, not riddles.

Bryn lay back on his pillow, and smiled with the satisfaction of having decided on his next move. He snuggled down under his duvet and closed his eyes as sleep took control.

The warmth was leaving the sun when Bryn woke up. He stretched his arms above his head, and looked in amazement at his bedside clock.

'I've been asleep for hours,' he said to Cadno, who pushed the door open and padded to the bed.

'How are you feeling?' said his grandfather, following the dog in to the bedroom.

'Fine now, Granddad. No shivers, don't feel cold.' Bryn

threw back the duvet. 'Think I'll get up. Have a wash and get dressed.' He grinned at his grandfather. 'But I'll still feel a little ill for mum, so she won't make me go to school tomorrow.'

Gareth winked. 'Reminds me of my own school days, Bryn. I was always looking for ways to skive off school.'

'Granddad,' said Bryn, swinging his legs out of the bed. 'Can I borrow your bible? I want to look something up.'

'Of course you can,' said Gareth. 'Maybe I can help. What exactly do you want to read?'

'I want to read all that "Revelation" bit, 'cos Miss Hughes seemed to know it from memory. She hardly looked at her book, and I saw a lot of the people in church also seemed to know it.'

'Can't remember that, Bryn.' Gareth sighed. 'Guess it's my age, though I do remember Selwyn coming and upsetting the vicar.' He turned to the door, clicking his fingers. Cadno looked up and followed. 'It's long past lunchtime, so I'll make us some hot soup. Give me a shout when you're dressed.'

Bryn dressed slowly and stared at himself in the mirror over the small chest of drawers. His face was very pale, and he pushed his hair out of his dull eyes. 'You look a sight,' he said to his reflection.

Why did horses come in the dream? I don't even like them. They're so big, and their teeth are large. I wouldn't let them take food from my hand like some folk. Too worried they'd bite a finger off. Now if I dreamed of dogs like Cadno, that would be different.

He stopped brushing his hair as a memory was recalled. But I did dream of Cadno, and it wasn't a nice dream either.

Bryn could smell the enticing aroma of vegetable soup as he descended the stairs. He walked to the kitchen and saw Gareth stirring something in a large saucepan.

'Sit yourself down, and I'll bring over the soup,' said Gareth, then pointed to a thick book on the table. 'I've marked the "Revelation" part in my bible, so you can read it, though why you find it interesting beats me.'

'Thanks, Granddad,' said Bryn, then held out his hands, a mischievous twinkle in his eyes. 'Washed 'em before I came down.'

Gareth turned, quickly scanned the upturned palms, then focussed on ladling out the soup. Bryn noticed his grandfather's shoulders shaking with quiet mirth. His eyes were laughing when he came to the table with the bowls of soup.

They looked at each other, and both burst out laughing. At that moment Bryn knew that he and grandfather had embarked on a new relationship. Barriers of age and views had been broken. In future, he was sure they would be friends. Granddad would give him the closeness and companionship he had lost, so long ago, with dad.

Bryn watched him place his glasses on his face, then reach for the bible. He flicked the pages until he reached the section where a red bookmark protruded. As he slowly consumed his soup, Gareth skipped through the 'Book of Revelation'.

''Can't understand why you're so interested, Bryn. It's all about the end of the world, as I see it. Hardly bedtime reading.'

'Not sure myself,' said Bryn and drank his soup, the warmth flowing though his body.

'That was great, Granddad. Thanks a lot.' Bryn wiped his mouth with his sleeve, and received raised eyebrows from Gareth, but no telling off.

'Do you think this is real, or is it just stories?' Bryn flicked through the pages, then stopped when he began to read 'Revelation Six'. He scanned through the sentences, picking out significant groups of words.

'I looked, and there before me was a white horse.' 'Then another horse came out, a fiery red one.' 'I looked, and there before me was a pale horse! Its rider was named Death, and

Hades was following close behind him.'

'What's the matter, Bryn?' said Gareth, seeing his grandson's face pale, and his hands trembling as they turned the pages.

'It's the horses. They were in my dream last night.'

'Not surprised. As I remember, your teacher was reading that part on Sunday, in church.'

'It's not just that, Granddad, there was something else.'

'So tell me.'

Before Bryn could reply, the shrill tones of the telephone interrupted the conversation. Gareth left the table, leaving his grandson reading the pages again. Nowhere was there any mention of a fiery sky, flames, and the ground burning furiously.

No, his dream had been something else, and he was involved in something awful yet to happen.

'Remember that man who gave you a lift home on Saturday?' said Gareth, coming back to the kitchen.

'Mr Holbrook?'

'That's right, Bob Holbrook. Anyway, he's invited you to play for one of his teams this Saturday. Said he'd pick you up about nine, as long as you're feeling better.'

Bryn's eyes lit up. His dream was consigned to the back of his mind, as he focussed on playing real football.

'That's fantastic. I'll be fine. Feeling better already.'

'So, you'll be able to go to school tomorrow?'

'Not sure I'll be that well,' grinned Bryn.

CHAPTER ELEVEN

Bryn was enjoying himself, and confidence increased as he found his footballing skills again. His sudden swerves on the left of the pitch had opponents sprawling. He was in his favourite position as a striker. As his left leg was the strongest, crossing the ball to the centre was becoming increasingly accurate.

When Bob arrived to pick him up, Bryn was ready, with his football kit in a small holdall. The only blot on the rising excitement as the week passed, happened when mother came home from work, the day he missed school.

She looked at him, felt his forehead, made him stick out his tongue, and took his temperature.

'Amazing recovery, young man, so tomorrow you can go to school.'

'Mum, I'm still feeling hot and shivery.'

'And I'm from the planet Mars,' said mother, the tone in her voice making it clear there would be no argument.

Bryn looked at grandfather for support, and was greeted with a slow shake of his head, and a broad grin.

All that was forgotten on Saturday morning. Bob had given one blast on his car horn, then opened the passenger door as

Bryn ran out of the cottage.

'Fit and well?'

'Great, Mr Holbrook. It'll be just great to be in a real match again.'

'I tried to get the village interested in having a boys' team, but since Mr Price has been teaching, the only game they want to know is Rugby. And then they have to play in the next village if they want a match. There's no pitch here.'

As they drove to town, Bryn learned that Bob was a qualified FA Coach, and had been helping BrynDewin Rangers football club for the past two years. They had several junior teams, playing in the local leagues, and Bryn would be playing for the third team, that afternoon.

'Got to start you somewhere, Bryn,' said Bob, then told him that his chance had come because several players were ill with flu. 'However, there is something which will please you.'

'What's that?'

'Our colours are black and white, the same as the "Rams".'

'We're bound to win then.'

Bryn had another surprise when Bob told him the name of his farm, 'Ffau-y-Cadno.'

'Fee what?'

Bob glanced at Bryn and smiled. 'I won't spell it for you, and I'm probably as good at speaking Welsh as you. Actually it means, "Fox Lair."'

'And have you any on your land?'

'I've not seen any,' said Bob, as he drove into the car park attached to the sports field. 'Have you?'

'No, but I've been told they were everywhere in Morredin, years ago.' Bryn decided not to say anymore about what he knew. He had something else on his mind.

He had flitted between tingling excitement and blood-chilling panic, that morning. It was almost a sense of foreboding that had nothing to do with the match, and it worried him.

Bob had introduced him to his team mates once they had entered the changing rooms in the clubhouse. Two other teams from the club had home fixtures, so a buzz of noise and activity had concentrated Bryn's mind.

He pulled on the kit, and grimaced when he saw the badge on his shirt was not the crest of Derby County. For one moment he felt despair, then it vanished when Bob called the team together for a tactical talk before the match began.

'Bethel Street Athletic are no push-overs, boys, so I want a hundred percent effort.'

Bryn listened to Bob with increasing self-doubt about his fitness. A few runs, and long walks with Cadno, was not a substitution for proper team training. He was aware the other members were casually glancing in his direction during Bob's pep talk.

'Right, then, BrynDewin Rangers. Go out and come in winners,' said Bob, then led the team out of the clubhouse.

As the game progressed, Bryn relaxed and began to enjoy himself. It's great to be back on a proper soccer pitch again, he thought, as he ran into position to receive passes.

Yeh! It's really something to feel my pace and the satisfaction of beating the other team. That's when I get the ball. Just wish the others would give me a chance to prove myself.

Bryn was still feeling full of energy when the whistle blew for half time. Neither side had scored, and the clubhouse was rapidly filling with tired footballers as whistles blew for a break in the other matches.

Plastic cups, full of water were handed out by Bob to his team. He gave another pep talk, and ended with, 'Bryn is spending too much time jogging up and down. I know he is new, but in this half, I want you to push the ball out to him more often. Let's give him a chance to show us what he can do.'

Bryn was happy, receiving the ball, side stepping opponents, running forwards, then crossing it to the centre. He found it frustrating that his team mates could not convert the chances into slamming the ball into the back of the Bethel Athletic net.

Bob was alternating between screaming from the touchline, and holding his head in his hands in despair. He glanced at his watch and noticed the seconds hand sweeping towards the end of the match.

'There's only fifteen minutes left. You should have been up by at least three,' he yelled through cupped hands. He knew his team could not hear his frustration, but voicing his annoyance helped him relax.

Bryn watched his opponent run towards him as he sped down the pitch, and decided to change tactics.

Instead of crossing the ball, he swerved inside the defender, and hurtled towards the goal. His speed, and sudden change of direction, fooled the opposition. They hesitated long enough for Bryn to jinx past another player, and position himself, with only the goalie to beat.

He pushed the ball to his trusty left foot, and balanced himself to shoot past the keeper into the top left hand corner. Then he hesitated.

Something made him lose concentration for a few seconds, and look at the faces of the small group standing behind the goal. Everything then appeared to go in slow motion, and the cries of the supporters were stilled. He seemed to have entered another dimension as he focussed on one figure.

His eyes widened, and the hairs stood erect on the back of his neck. The vague outline of a tall man with a craggy face topped with a mop of thick black hair was familiar.

Large, round eyes were dark pools of merriment.

Bryn faltered in mid stride, as he heard the shouts of the watchers again. He tamely punted the ball to the goalkeeper as he mouthed, 'Dad.'

He stood still, ignoring the anger of his team, and the relieved laughter of their opponents. His body trembled with the shock, but when he looked up again, the man had vanished.

'I know I saw him,' he said aloud.

'Saw who?' said an irate Rangers player. 'All you had to do was tap the ball past the goalie, and the match was ours. You're useless, utterly useless.'

As if to reinforce the anger, the referee blew his whistle to end the game. The players trooped off the field, and Bryn was left to slouch slowly back to the dressing rooms on his own. He occasionally turned his head to glance at the spectators, but could not see the familiar face.

'I did see him,' he said as he clumped up the stairs to enter the building. 'He was there.'

'Who, Bryn?' said Bob. 'Who did you see, so important, you missed an easy goal?'

'My dad. Daft, I know, 'cos I've not seen him in years. Anyway, he lives in Derby, so how could he know I was playing here today?'

'I have no idea what you're talking about, but you have given me problems now. It's going to be hard to persuade the others to accept you in the team again.'

'Sorry, Mr Holbrook,' said Bryn, and shuffled into the dressing room. He stared at the floor so that he could not see the hostility in the faces of the other boys. Their angry comments could not be screened from his burning ears.

Bryn towelled himself dry, unwilling to accompany the others into the showers.

I've let everyone down, he thought, slowly dressing. But

I'm sure it was dad out there, or was it? Was I seeing things 'cos I wished he had been there to see me play? Mr Holbrook must be real mad at me, letting him down. Fancy missing a sitter like that! What a prat I must have looked out there.

'Ready, Bryn?' said Bob, his face blank, and voice cold.

'Yes, and I'm sorry I let you down.'

'Never mind me, Bryn. You not only let me down, but your teammates as well.'

He led the way out of the sportsground, and unlocked his car. 'Get in, Bryn, and maybe you can explain on the way home why you ruined a good display by one minute's lapse of concentration.'

Bryn was silent as the car cruised along the winding road from town. He was in turmoil with his thoughts, thinking about the easy goal he missed, then the vision of his father at the match.

'Care to explain what happened back there?' said Bob.

'I thought I saw dad standing behind the goal, just as I was about to shoot.'

'And?'

'But it couldn't have been him, 'cos I've not seen him in years.'

'Maybe he just happened to be at the sports ground.'

'He still lives in Derby, so why should he happen to be in BrynDewen when I'm playing there?'

'And that's why you missed that easy goal?'

Bryn nodded, then leaned back in his seat. 'Do you think that, maybe it was 'cos I was thinking that I wished dad could see me playing today, I, sort of, made him be there?'

'Probably, Bryn, unless,' Bob smiled, 'it was a "Doppelgänger."'

'A what-er?'

'It means someone who is the spilt image of yourself. There's a theory that all of us have someone living somewhere who look just like ourselves, and they don't have to be related.'

'So you think that I might have seen this Doppel thing?'

'Possible, Bryn. But I wouldn't like to have to explain to the other lads that was the reason you missed that goal.'

'Won't happen again, Mr Holbrook.'

'Somehow I don't think it will,' said Bob as he halted his car outside the cottage. 'And I like to be called 'Bob' by my friends. You played well, apart from that one incident. I can see why Derby took an interest in you.'

'Can I train with the Rangers then?'

'Ask your mum, and if she says "Yes," I'll pick you up a week tomorrow.'

Bob watched Bryn open his door and leave the car. 'I'll phone this evening to see what she says.'

Bryn watched the car drive away, then turned as Cadno rushed at him, barking happily. Gareth was standing in the doorway.

'How did it go?'

'Not bad, Granddad,' said Bryn, kneeling down to receive the affections of his dog. 'Missed a sitter though. No excuses, just a stupid miskick.'

'But apart from that, you enjoyed the game?'

Bryn nodded, and looked round for his mother. He made the excuse for missing the goal, on impulse.

I don't think Granddad would understand this dopple thing any more than I do, he thought. Best keep it to myself.

'Mum out shopping?'

'Should be home soon. Would you like a sandwich to keep you going until supper? Bet you've not eaten since breakfast.'

'Thanks, Granddad,' said Bryn, climbing the stairs to his room. There was something he wanted to look at.

He pulled his notebook out from its hiding place, then

turned to the last page. Between it and the cover was a photograph. Bryn stared at the picture of the man with a young boy on his shoulders. Both were laughing.

As he looked at the familiar face of his father, Bryn heard a soft chuckle behind him. There was menace in the tone, and an icy chill filled the room.

He turned round but there was no one there, not even his doppelgänger.

.

CHAPTER TWELVE

B ryn ran along the side of the swirling stream, which bounced over the stones, and tumbled down small waterfalls on its journey. Cadno bounded ahead, ears flat and tail streaming behind his lean body. The morning sun streamed down, warming the autumnal day, brightening the changing colours of the leaves on the distant trees.

Granddad had added his support when Bryn asked his mother if he could join the football club.

'Do him good to meet some new boys, and train with them.'

'Even though they meet on a Sunday morning?'

'That is a pity,' said Gareth, then winked at Bryn. 'But the Lord does move in mysterious ways.'

Bryn was quiet as he laid the table for supper, thinking about the frightening chuckle he had heard in his bedroom. Something important was happening to him. Too many voices in his head, too many nightmares. What was the purpose Selwyn predicted had brought him to Morredin?

'So when would this Bob want you to start with the club?'

'A week tomorrow, Mum. He'd pick me up, and bring me

home as the buses are lousy on a Sunday.'

'They're not very good in the week either,' she said, filling three plates with a mouth-watering meal. Carrying the plates to the table, she sat down with her father and Bryn. They watched as she poured herself some water from a jug.

'I suppose if your grandfather isn't shocked that you want to play football on a Sunday, then I can't really object.'

'Does that mean I can tell Mr Holbrook it's okay for next week?'

'Yes,' said his mother, then was surprised by Bryn leaving his place and throwing his arms round her and shouting, 'You're the best mum in the world.'

Yeah, she is, thought Bryn as he jogged along the path. His pace was relaxed and a gentle breeze ensured conditions were good for a run.

I'll make it up to Bob for that stupid miss, just 'cos I thought I saw a dopperwanger, or whatever it is. Good old granddad, being on my side.

'Know what, Cadno?' Bryn said aloud. 'He's not as bad as I thought. I just wish that…' His voice faded as his father's face appeared in his thoughts. What a pity dad hadn't been there to see me play.

But he wasn't at the match, and I made a complete idiot of myself missing that easy goal.

Bryn saw the peaks of Court of Foxes, and without thinking, turned off the path and began working his way through the scrub on its rising sides. He was happy, and his legs felt strong as he jogged over the rough grass and jumped over the rocky outcrops. He followed a rough track, indicated by a flattening of the grass.

Running was laboured as the slope of the hill increased, and the ground became rough and uneven.

'I'm not as fit as I thought, Cadno,' puffed Bryn, and wiped sweat from his forehead with a hand. 'This sun's quite hot, which doesn't help matters.'

Cadno stopped some way up the hill, looked down at his young master and barked his annoyance at the delay.

'It's all right for you, but I've not been up this high before.' Bryn slumped down on the ground, his chest heaving with the exertion. 'Anyway, you've got four legs.' He looked down the way they had come. The stream was just a winding silver snake, glistening in the sun, and the village houses were as small as the pieces in the Monopoly game.

'We've climbed a long way. No wonder I'm shattered.' Bryn twisted his head and frowned as he noticed a beaten uphill path to his left. It skirted the hillside, and disappeared round a huge crop of boulders.

'That's odd. Looks like it's been used for some time,' said Bryn, getting to his feet. Cadno stood, with lolling tongue and bright eyes. He was trembling with the expectation that the rest was over and he could run ahead once more.

'Wonder where that leads?' said Bryn, but a nagging thought was already infiltrating his mind. The words of granddad came back, telling of a procession in the middle of the night climbing this hill.

An enveloping fear of what he might see could not stop Bryn working his way round the hillside. He was driven by a power too strong to combat. The sun changed, becoming brighter, and deep red in colour. Its beaming light flooded the ground below, which took on the colour of...

'Blood,' whispered Bryn, as memories of his last nightmare gave crystal clear visions in his minds eye.

His imagination heard whispering from behind the rocks, as though unseen people were watching his every step. A breeze tumbled down the hill, increasing in strength. Bryn cried out as the rocks changed colour in the sun. His nightmare was becoming a reality.

He stumbled and looked upwards, expecting the red clouds

to part and reveal a horse prancing though the sky. Cadno had slowed and walked warily by Bryn's side. He seemed to be conscious that something was wrong, and his hackles were raised, and ears pricked to listen to every sound.

'What's happening, Cadno? You know something's wrong, don't you?' Bryn wanted to turn back, but was urged by a force he could not control to continue. Cadno disappeared behind a huge rocky outcrop, then Bryn's blood was chilled.

A howl, soft at first, then increasing in intensity, shattered the quietness. It bounced around the hillside, and Bryn imagined that other howls joined in.

'Cadno!' cried Bryn, and forced his tired legs to run along the track, round the rocky outcrop, until he reached an oasis of grass in a small hollow. Cadno sat in the grass, and stopped howling when he saw his master.

Bryn ignored his dog as something else attracted his attention. In the centre of the hollow, as though thrown there by some giant, was a huge flat boulder. The top surface looked as though some extra large chisel had been used to flatten and smooth the black rock.

The sun's rays coned into a beam of light that connected the stone with the heavens, giving the boulder the appearance of a ghostly structure. Bryn sank to his knees, overcome by a powerful energy that seethed in the hollow. This was a special place, known to only a few.

'Something horrible happens here,' he whispered, shivering despite his sweaty face. 'That looks like an altar.'

His imagination saw a priest with a huge curved knife ready to plunge it into the body of a terrified man, stretched out on the huge stone. His arms and legs were held by assistants wearing black robes, their faces hidden by masks.

'They sacrifice people here,' he whispered, and was answered by the crash of thunder above him. The red clouds thickened, and he cowered on the grass, waiting for the deluge of blood to engulf him.

Nothing happened. No deluge of rain, or anything. Just the crashing of thunder in the blood-red sky, and the crackling of mysterious energy in the hollow.

'What's happening?' he cried. 'What is this place?' Then, not knowing why he asked, Bryn said, 'What do you want with me?'

No one answered, but the thunder ceased, to be replaced by the rustling of a breeze that grew louder. As the noise increased, Bryn could hear it change to the sound of a multitude of voices.

He threw himself on the ground and covered his ears with his hands to try and block out the voices that said one word, over and over again.

'Adentium, adentium, adentium,' said the unseen chorus, and Cadno crawled to his master and whimpered by his side.

Then all was peaceful. The voices were stilled, the gentle breeze returned, and even the sun was restored to its yellowish colour.

Bryn kneeled in the grass and looked at the boulder. No longer bathed in sunlight, it just had the appearance of a huge black rock. He slowly walked to the stone and ran his hand along the rough surface. It was warm from the sun's rays, and Bryn was surprised to feel the smoothness on the flat top.

'What happened just now?' he asked Cadno, who ran to the top of the hollow, and barked. 'That's not just any old rock, Cadno. Something happens here, and it's not nice either.'

Cadno cocked his head to one side, and listened with erect ears. He barked again, as if to tell his young master it was time to have more exercise.

'I just wish I had some of your energy, then I'd show 'em at the next match.' Bryn climbed out of the hollow and began the long descent, watching Cadno hurtle down the slope.

When he reached the junction with the track down to the stream, Bryn saw the familiar figure of Selwyn. His thick tangled mass of hair wafted round his face in the breeze, and his eyes were stern as they viewed the oncoming Bryn.

'I heard the thunder, and yet no rain came. I knew the forces were gathering in the hills.'

'What forces?'

'What did you see, Bryn?'

'I came across a weird huge flat stone back there, in a hollow.'

'What else did you see?'

'Nothing 'cept...'

'Tell me.'

'Sounds daft, but the sun and clouds turned red, and it looked just like a huge torch as it lit up the stone.'

'Ah,' sighed Selwyn, then came forward and placed a hand under Bryn's chin. He tilted his face so that he could look into his eyes. 'Tell me all that happened back there, Bryn. Leave nothing out, even if it seems unimportant to you.'

'You'll think me crazy if I tell you everything I think has happened.'

'Maybe what your mind tells you could not possibly happen, in reality is a fact.'

'Selwyn, will you please stop talking in riddles,' said Bryn, watching Cadno chase a rabbit ahead of them.

'I do not think your brain is playing you tricks, Bryn. I believe you are like a...,how can I explain in simple terms?' Selwyn stopped walking and stroked his beard. He was silent for a moment, then smiled. 'Ah, now I have an analogy. A radio, or television picks up unseen signals from the air around us. Then, by some miracle, we hear voices and see pictures.'

'How did you know I hear voices?' whispered Bryn.

'You-hear-voices?' said Selwyn, slowly.

'Yeah. Do you think I'm going mad or something?'

'Alas, no, my young friend. What you say gives me great cause for concern, and trepidation.'

'You're talking in riddles again.'

Selwyn did not reply at first. He turned right at a large boulder, with a small bush precariously living in a crack on top. Waving Bryn to follow, he strode across the hillside.

'Where are we going?' said Bryn, trotting to keep up with the striding man.

'To my home, Bryn. I think we need to talk.'

Bryn hesitated, and Cadno ran back to his side, and sat down.

'What is the problem?' said Selwyn.

'It's just that…'

'You have been told not to go to my home. It is dangerous, and who knows what may befall you?' Selwyn chuckled. 'You may never be seen again.'

'Why don't people like you? Don't see why I was told by Carys and the others not to go to your home. Mind you, they did say that if I saw your place, I'd know why you're called the "mad monk".

Selwyn threw back his head and bellowed with laughter. His whole body shook with mirth, and tears rolled down his face.

'I do not laugh at you, my friend, but at what the others have said.' Selwyn wiped his face with a sleeve, then, still chuckling, motioned with his staff for Bryn to follow. 'You must judge for yourself when you see my home. There is a saying, "Do not judge a book by its cover", and there is great wisdom in those words.'

'I'm sure you're right,' said Bryn, thinking that he really hadn't a clue what the old man meant.

They walked down the hillside, and eventually came to the path by the stream. Selwyn lead the way to the stepping stones. The ground, through the wood, was carpeted with moss, fallen leaves and twigs, and the occasional branch of an ageing tree.

Bryn marvelled at the banners of sunlight streaming through the trees, creating pools of bright gold on the floor. He felt peaceful walking through the wood, and Cadno would dart from side to side, nose to the ground, picking up new and interesting scents.

Selwyn strode ahead, using his staff to lengthen his stride. He was silent, and Bryn could see that they were using a well-worn path between the trees. Time meant nothing in that enchanted place, and Bryn was sorry when they finally emerged to be confronted by a small stone cottage.

It was sitting on the hillside surrounded by a dry stone wall, which had tumbled down in places. Gateposts of larger stones held the remains of a wooden gate, which leaned against one post. A track lead from the entrance, going behind the cottage, and joined a road further up the hill.

'There is the home of the "mad monk", and where terrible things happen,' Selwyn turned his head to beam at Bryn, 'if you believe everything you hear about me.'

As they crossed the ground to reach the cottage, Bryn's eyes widened in amazement. It wasn't just the gateposts that had writing in red paint. The whole cottage and the roof were similarly decorated with inscriptions.

Selwyn strode through the entrance in the stone wall, and Bryn stopped to read the messages on the posts. They did not make sense.

One post bore the inscription, 'And he shall send his angels with a great sound,' and the other, seemingly one of Selwyn's riddles. 'A whip for the horse. A bridle for the Ass and a rod for the fool's back.'

Bryn stood in front of the house and gazed in shock. All the messages were either friendly, 'Blessed is he who considers the poor,' or frightening, 'The vengeance of eternal fire.' The vivid red paint shouted the importance of the writing.

'Come inside, my young friend, and I will get us some sustenance to refresh our weary bodies,' said Selwyn, and pushed open the front door, which was badly in need of a coat or two of paint.

'Okay,' said Bryn, and casually scrutinised the small garden. He realised that Selwyn did not grow much apart from rows of vegetables. The rest of the ground was covered in unloved, rough grass, badly in need of mowing. Bushes of varying types crowded the ground to the back, and dandelions and other weeds flourished happily.

As he followed Selwyn inside, Bryn noticed a small brick shed tacked on to the side of the cottage. A family of moss was growing vigorously on the corrugated roof.

What a dump, thought Bryn. Who, in their right mind, would want to live in this hole? Miles from anywhere, bet there isn't any electricity. Then he noticed the wall lamps, and the ceiling fixture. He moved his hand to a wall switch, and the room was clearly visible as the lamps were turned on.

'I'll make us some tea,' said Selwyn from another room. 'Do you like chocolate biscuits?'

'Thanks,' said Bryn as he wandered round the room. The stone floor had some faded small carpets scattered in a vain attempt to cover the surface. One wall had a bookcase stretching from floor to ceiling, and a heavy table occupied the centre. Three chairs and a stool were placed nearby, and a comfortable-looking armchair had been placed near the black fireplace. A large telescope was aimed through a window at the distant hills.

A log fire glowed in the grate, sparks and smoke rising lazily up the wide stone-built chimney. The room was warm and comfortable, and Cadno quickly found the source of the heat. With a sigh, he stretched in front of the fire and closed his eyes.

'Pull up that stool and sit by the fire,' said Selwyn, entering from the kitchen. He carried a tray with two steaming mugs and a tin of biscuits. Placing it on the table, he went to a large wooden chest and pulled back the lid. Inside it was filled with logs, and he took out two pieces of sawn branch and pushed them into the fire.

Cadno lifted his head as the wood caught fire and crackled, then let it flop back on the floor.

Selwyn gave one mug to Bryn, watching him take a biscuit from the tin. He placed it carefully between his teeth, then carried the mug and stool to the fireside.

'Before I talk, I suppose you wonder, assuming you noticed, why I have painted words all over my home.'

'Noticed?' said Bryn. 'Could hardly miss it, and-yeah-was...,wondering why.'

'Do you believe in God?'

'Not sure,' said Bryn, chewing slowly. 'Certainly don't believe in angels and things. Anyway, where's heaven supposed to be?'

'A good question, and one I cannot answer, never having been there myself.' Selwyn supped noisily from his mug, then looked at his guest.

'Let me put this another way, in such a manner as you might, hopefully, understand the question easier. Do you believe in good and evil?'

'Yeah,' said Bryn, and gave a piece of his biscuit to Cadno. 'But I don't believe in monsters, and devils, and things like that.' He took a sip from his mug, then screwed up his face.

'There's no sugar in it. It's 'orrible.'

'To drink tea without sugar brings out the full flavour of the leaves. That is one reason, and the other reason you should know. Sugar is bad for your teeth.'

Selwyn watched Bryn take another sip, then pull an even worse expression. With a deep sigh, the old man left his armchair and walked to his kitchen. He returned with a small pot of sugar and a spoon.

Leaning over Bryn, he smiled and said, 'One or two spoonfuls, young sir?'

'Two, please,' said Bryn, then waited until the sugar had been stirred, and took a mouthful. 'Much better, thanks.'

'Now then, we were discussing good and evil, my cottage, and Morredin.' Selwyn sat in the armchair and smiled at Cadno who was snoring happily in his sleep.

'He is lucky, not having to worry about such things. You may remember the first time we met, I had a strong feeling that fate had brought you here. Events since, have strengthened that feeling, but…' Selwyn stared into the fire. 'At the moment I am not sure of your role in life here. Who or what is God is a matter of debate. After all,' he smiled, 'there is argument as to whether God is a "he" or a "her". But you and I can agree that there are forces for good and forces for evil. Unfortunately, in my view, the forces of evil are alive and kicking in our world, and there are those who pray to that evil.'

'Is that why you have painted messages on your home?' said Bryn. "cos I noticed there are nice messages and some frightening.'

'Well perceived, my young friend. I am trying to give a warning to all my visitors that we have a choice in life. When I came here, I quickly picked up signals that evil flourished in Morredin. There is a history of strange events, with sights in the sky that should not happen…'

'Like me seeing the sun and clouds go red?'

'Yes.'

'I saw it in a nightmare a couple of days ago,' said Bryn, and walked over to the table to take another biscuit. 'Did bad people kill prisoners on that stone hundreds of years ago?'

'No, Bryn, but its name is important.'

'And?'

'Its called "Craig y Dewin,"'

'Creeg a what?'

'Wizard's rock.'

CHAPTER THIRTEEN

Bryn stared at Selwyn. 'Wizard's rock?' He sipped his tea, screwing up his face in concentration. 'Has it anything to with that man who's buried in the churchyard? 'cos I seem to remember being told he was a wizard by granddad.'

'That would appear to be truth of the matter, Bryn.'

'So what did he do up there? Pray? Cast spells, whatever that's supposed to be?'

'There are many stories about Emrys Morgan. As to what he could do in the way of magic, I am not sure. It is said he could change from man to animal or bird. Stories abound about his powers to make changes to the weather at will. But I am sure he did pray on that altar, for that is what that stone was used for.'

'But he didn't pray to God, did he'

'No,' whispered Selwyn, and stared into the fire.

'Who then?'

'The "Great Dragon", and all his evil.' Selwyn walked over to an old wooden chest of drawers and pulled out a well -used bible. He turned pages, then walked back with the open book to his armchair and sat down.

'The section called "Revelation" would appear to hold the answers to much of what happened, and still happens, here,' said Selwyn, tapping the pages. 'When I came here, I was aware, as I think I told you, that there was an undercurrent of evil living in Morredin. Don't ask me how I knew, Bryn. I just sensed it. I could smell evil. And that evil knew I was a danger. It showed itself in many ways and even now works through many people who live here.'

'Granddad told me that when he was my age, he would see people making their way up the Court of Foxes at night. He knows something, but won't talk about it.' Bryn walked to Selwyn's side and looked down at the open bible. 'Do you mean there's people walking round with "666" showing under their hair, like in 'The Omen'?'

'The Omen? Do you mean the film?'

'It was real spooky. Saw it on the telly.'

Selwyn flicked through the pages then stopped and pointed. 'This you will find of interest.'

He began to read. 'This comes from "Revelation 13", and talks about a beast coming out of the sea. However, this is where your film got its numbers from. At the end it says this, 'If anyone has insight, let him calculate the number of the beast, for it is man's number. His number is 666."

'So what does that mean?'

'Not sure myself, Bryn,' smiled Selwyn. 'But I don't think it means you have to look under the hair of everyone you suspect.'

'Looked good in the film though.' Bryn knelt down by the old man, and the visions of his encounter on the hill were clear in his memory. 'But the horses, red sky and the other things are in that bible, aren't they?'

'Yes.'

'Do you believe everything that's written there?'

Selwyn stroked his beard. 'I believe there are truths in

those words, even though sometimes it does not make sense. In the same way that I believe that Satan, called the "Great Dragon" here, does exist and can take human form.'

'Yeah, but you don't believe this, do you?' said Bryn tapping a page. He then read out, 'And I saw a beast coming out of the sea. He had ten horns and seven heads, What a load of rubbish.'

'Maybe,' said Selwyn. 'But then, maybe such horrors can be conjured by those with the power of evil.' He turned back a few pages and quietly read aloud, 'The Great Dragon" was hurled down, that ancient serpent called the devil or Satan.' He paused, then read very slowly. 'He was hurled to the earth and his angels with him.'

'Are you saying…?'

'Yes, Bryn. I am saying I believe that Emrys Morgan was one of the evil spirits cast out of heaven, and his evil powers are here. His disciples believe he will come back and resurrect the "Great Dragon", Who would believe that Satan would choose a little village in Wales to finally reveal himself?'

'And you think that some of the people here are, sort of, devils?'

'Not devils as such, Bryn. Though I think that the powers of evil have taken over families in this area, and the soul of Emrys Morgan is, even now, among us, watching, waiting. After all, his name does mean immortal in welsh.'

Selwyn bent down to place a hand on Bryn's shoulder. He voiced his concern as he saw Bryn pale and his body tremble.

'What is the matter? What is it I have said that troubles you?'

'Saying that Emrys Morgan is here.' Bryn looked up, tears filling his eyes. "cos I think I've…heard him. He talks to me in my nightmares. I'm sure I've seen his ghost as well.'

Thunder crashed down from the surrounding hills and echoed through the valleys. Lightning hissed and sizzled like a huge fireworks display. The sky rapidly blackened, and then the rain came. Gallons of water hurtled down in sheets that bounced off the ground and created a mist that swallowed the paths, tracks and hills. It beat a loud tattoo on the roof, and the lights flickered on and off.

Cadno trembled as the thunder rolled round the Court of Foxes. Selwyn walked to the window and watched the deluge. He sighed, then turned his head to look at Bryn.

'That is not a normal storm, to come so suddenly with no warning.'

'What are you saying?'

'I believe it is Dyn Hysbys telling us he is here, watching and warning us. It worries me that more signs are appearing to show his evil is ready.' Selwyn listened as hailstones hit the roof, the drumming of their impact sounding like hundreds of charging horses.

A window exploded and the glass showered into the room, followed by hailstones the size of golf balls. Cadno howled and crept under the table. Bryn yelled and threw himself on the floor. Selwyn faced the howling wind that hurtled through the shattered window, his white hair streaming behind his head.

'In the name of the Supreme Goodness, I command you to leave us.' Selwyn raised his arms above his head, and his voice boomed with authority.

As suddenly as it appeared, the thunder ceased, along with the wind and hailstones. Water dripped off the roof, splashing into the large pools surrounding the cottage. The sun drifted out from behind a cloud, and bathed the cottage and the hills in warmth.

Selwyn watched the steam rising from the ground, then turned round to face his visitor.

'I think you were supposed to be out there, Bryn. It worries me that your coming to Morredin has begun a chain of events we cannot stop.'

'Who are you?' whispered Bryn. He stood up and stared at the broken glass covering the floor. 'How did you make it stop? Have you powers like that Emrys Morgan? Are you a wizard?'

Selwyn sighed, and was silent as he placed another log on the fire. 'No, Bryn, I am not a wizard, and do not possess powers myself, but know how to summon the power of the Supreme Goodness. As for who I am, that is simple. I am a mere human like yourself, but something happened many years ago, which I shall impart to you one day. However, I am increasingly persuaded that you have the power to either stop, or release the devil's evil that would conquer the world, and…' He picked up his bible and scanned the pages. 'You scoffed at the description of the beast, but listen to this, Bryn.'

The old man coughed, then began to read. 'All inhabitants of the earth will worship the beast.' He placed the bible on the table. 'There is something else that persuades me this small village was chosen for the resurrection of Satan. You have remarked on the fact that 7 December was both the birth date, and the date of the death of Emrys Morgan.'

Bryn felt cold, and the hairs on the back of his neck stood erect as he waited for Selwyn to continue.

'We can also read in "The Book of Revelations" several references to the number seven. For example, revelation five says, "a scroll sealed with seven seals". Then there are the "seven thunders," the beast had seven heads and there are the seven bowls of God's wrath.' Selwyn looked up and said, 'Did you know you will not find any building in Morredin numbered seven?'

'No, but what do you mean by "resurrection"?'

'It means, bringing back to life, and I suspect that…'

'Selwyn, I have a secret which worries me.'

'And what is this terrible secret?'

'It's just that I have the same birthday as Emrys Morgan, 7 December.'

There, he'd said it. Got it off his chest. Glad he'd told Selwyn first. It had been playing on his mind ever since he visited the grave of Emrys Morgan. At first it had been a surprise, now it was becoming almost frightening. He was probably being silly, but felt more relaxed now he had told the old man.

Selwyn was silent as he went to a cupboard and took out a broom and dustpan. He began to sweep up the broken glass, which tinkled as the small pieces were piled up. Bryn took the dustpan and knelt down and watched the old man's face as he brushed the pile into the plastic container. The wrinkled face betrayed nothing.

'There,' said Selwyn, taking the full pan from Bryn. 'I'll just empty this in the bin outside then get some wood and cover the broken window.'

'So what do you think about my birthday being the same as this Emrys Morgan?'

'There should be something I can use in the shed,' said Selwyn, and opened the door. He walked outside, followed by Bryn and Cadno, and emptied the contents of the dustpan into a battered dustbin. Selwyn then opened the door to the small shed.

Bryn was surprised to see a small diesel generator in one corner, and several full containers of fuel. The generator was thumping with regular beats, and Selwyn pulled out a dipstick from the side, and nodded his satisfaction.

'You see, I might be some way from Morredin, but there is no reason why I should not have electricity. On the other side of the cottage I have bottled gas for cooking.'

'Selwyn, about my birthday. Do you think…?'

'Ah, this old wood panel should cover the window for the time being,' said Selwyn, and picked up an old piece of plywood from the floor. He blew away the dust, and knocked two small spiders to the floor.

'Come, Bryn, let us get that window covered.'

Bryn walked behind him as they left the shed and wandered back to the cottage. He realised that Selwyn would not, for reasons of his own, discuss the coincidence of his birthday having the same date as Emrys Morgan. Bryn noticed Selwyn's face when he told him his secret. It registered shock at the news.

He glanced at the open pages of the bible as Selwyn picked up a hammer and gradually nailed the plywood over the gaping hole. The rhythmic sound of hammer on nail was broken by a muttered oath when Selwyn missed the nail and hit his fingers instead.

'If this Emrys Morgan was Satan's servant, then what stopped him doing the terrible things it says here?'

'By being destroyed the only way he and his devils can be stopped. It seems he came home one night, very much the worse for drink. He went to bed, and in his drunken state knocked over a large candle.

'Emrys never woke up, and the candle set fire to his room, then the whole mansion caught fire. His servants ran for their lives, and when the flames died down, the mansion was destroyed. The fires of hell were his destruction. What remained of Emrys was burnt beyond recognition.'

'But you say he, or rather his ghost, still lives here,' said Bryn.

'I do believe that is the truth,' said Selwyn, fingering his beard. He muttered to himself, and motioned Bryn to sit down. A final nail was hammered into the temporary repair, then the old man sat in his place by the fire. He extended his hands to warm them in the heat from the crackling flames.

'Bryn, I think I will tell you more about myself, and why I am increasingly worried about events.' He stared into the fire for a moment, sighed, and leaned back.

'When I was much younger, I came to Wales to climb Snowdon. In those days I was an officer in the Army, and reached the rank of Major. Life was good, and I lived well, as apart from my Army pay, my background allowed me to have more money from the family wealth.'

Selwyn closed his eyes and smiled. 'Oh, yes, Bryn, I thought my future was going to be a life of adventure, fun, and living well. But fate had other ideas.'

'What happened?' whispered Bryn.

'As I said, my world was turned upside down on that fateful day when I was on Snowdon. It was winter, and there had been a heavy fall of snow. But I wasn't worried, as I was a competent climber, and my two Army companions were very experienced.

'We were not roped together as the slope was not too steep. The sun was shining, and the snow firm. But I slipped, and as I fell on my back, something made the snow move like an avalanche. Faster and faster I slid, desperately trying to halt my tumble, with the snow now roaring down the mountain.' Selwyn shook as the memory of the terror was relived. 'My companions could only look as I disappeared over the edge of the rock face in a torrent of snow. They must have thought that I was bound to be killed.'

'What happened?'

'As I tumbled down the mountain, terrified as my speed increased, I remember screaming out for help. I was sure I was facing death. Then I heard a voice above me saying, "take my hand"'. The voice repeated those words over and over again until, without thinking, I stretched an arm above my head.' Selwyn looked at Bryn. 'I did not believe in miracles until then. A strong hand reached down and grasped mine.

My descent was halted, and I found myself being slowly dragged up the mountain. Up and up I was hauled until I found myself on a ledge with a small cave behind.

When I looked round to thank my saviour, there was no one there. Not even an imprint of feet, never mind the signs of a human form, in the snow.'

'How were you found?'

'I was on the ledge all night, and that small cave probably saved me from freezing to death. My friends had obviously climbed down and raised the alarm. At first light, a helcopter was flying round, and must have seen the sun flashing from a small mirror I used to attract their attention. Later, a rescue team reached me, and guided me down to safety. I didn't tell them of my miracle, Bryn, because I knew they would have thought me demented. They were persuaded that I had been lucky to tumble on to the ledge.'

'That's an amazing story, but what's it got to do with Morredin?'

'It was not the end of my adventures with a force greater than man. You must understand that, as an Army man, I was trained to look for the obvious, understandable and explainable. What happened to me on that mountain could not be explained. Not with earthly reasoning anyway.'

Bryn looked at Selwyn, who was staring at the fire, eyes ablaze with excitement as he relived his past. The old man sighed, then smiled at his visitor. He tapped the open bible a few times.

'There is more truth written in that book about the relation between heaven and hell and man than I realised.'

'So you do believe in God?'

'Not sure, my young friend. Certainly I cannot conceive the picture of an old man with a long flowing beard, sitting on some heavenly throne.'

'So if he doesn't look like you, what does he look like?'

'God knows,' chuckled, Selwyn. 'But of one thing I am sure. Whatever form the Supreme Goodness takes, it would never be the nightmare monstrosities of the Great Dragon and his acolytes.'

'Selwyn?'

'Yes, Bryn?'

'Will you, please, speak in words I understand.'

'Of course I will. Now then, just what word do you not perceive?'

'There you go again. What's this perceive?'

'Simple enough word, means understand.'

'So can you tell me, in simple words, what acolyte means?'

'Follower, disciple, believer, apostle.'

Bryn stroked his dog and thought that he would always have difficulty in understanding everything Selwyn said. Maybe it was the way all grown-ups talked.

'So what adventures did you have after that mountain story, 'cos I'm not sure if I believe you.'

'It happened, Bryn, believe me. Afterwards I read the bible, and that same voice told me I had been chosen for a mission. I was not told the mission, but knew I had to devote my life to it. So I resigned my commission and left the Army.'

Selwyn left his chair and threw another log on the fire, then turned to face Bryn. He took the bible from him, and his hands were shaking as he placed it on the table.

'Every time I placed the bible down and opened it, some force made me turn to "Revelations". And reading the story of the fight between Good and Evil made me realise that was my destiny. I had to look for signs of the Great Dragon, and fight him and his followers.'

'So how did you know where to go?'

'I didn't for some years. In fact, my friend,' Selwyn stroked his beard and chuckled. 'I did become a monk, thinking this was my destiny

'A monk?' Bryn's eyes widened in astonishment.

'But not a mad one, I hasten to say,' said Selwyn. 'But the voice made me study "Revelations" in depth, and then, one day, it all came to me.' The old man sighed. 'So much wandering to find the truth. A truth that stares us in the face in that holy book.'

'You're talking in riddles again.'

'Not when all becomes clear, Bryn.' Selwyn turned the pages of his worn bible, and read one sentence. 'I saw in the right hand of him who sat on the throne a scroll with writing on both sides and sealed with seven seals.'

'And?'

'There is such a scroll, or maybe now in the form of a book, and the holder could bring the destruction of the world we know, and the powers of evil in control. The Great Dragon, or Satan as he is usually known, would be King on earth and all would bend the knee to him. I believe his acolyte Emrys Morgan had that evil, terrible scroll, and was waiting for the message from his master.'

'What message?'

'To open the seven seals, and with the power of the prayers and magic contained within those pages, bring his master to earth. The Great Dragon would appear, and all hell, literally, would be let loose.

'So where is this scroll thing now?'

'I believe it is still here, somewhere. I do not believe it was burnt with Emrys Morgan in his mansion. I believe his followers fervently pray the book will be found, the seals broken, and they will rule the world. As I told you before, Bryn, do not believe all you see and hear. Things, and people, are not what they seem. Evil abounds here. It is like a sleeping snake, waiting to wake up and strike.' Selwyn gently placed the bible on the table.

'I left the monastery because I suddenly realised the mission my voice had set me. It was to search, and find, the scroll with seven seals before the evil forces. I returned to Wales, as my Army trained mind suggested this being where I had been saved, here I should begin my search. The evil I felt when reaching Morredin was like an enveloping, choking cloud. The book of evil is here, Bryn.'

Bryn stared at the lights as they flickered. His mind was in turmoil as the memories of his dreams tumbled out. He seemed to be searching for something in that mysterious cave. Surely he couldn't be looking for this scroll thing. He didn't even know it existed until just now.

'I found a cave which was weird. It looked like it was used for some sort of meeting.'

'I know that cave, Bryn, and those who use it. Some are true believers in the Great Dragon, and others think it just a joke and a bit of fun.' Selwyn looked at a clock on the wall over the fireplace. 'Dear, dear. Just look at the time. I think we have spoken for long enough, and your dog looks restless.'

'Mum will kill me,' said Bryn, glancing at the clock. 'I promised I'd be home by half past one, as she's cooking.'

'We shall talk again, now I have told you so much. But I cannot entreat you enough, not to talk about our conversation with anyone.'

'Not even granddad or mum?'

'No one,' said Selwyn. He led the way to the door, and placed a hand on Bryn's shoulder. 'I do not yet understand the importance of your presence in all this. But of this I am sure. You are an important piece in the jigsaw, which I believe is fast becoming completed. Be careful, my young friend, because if I realise your importance, so do others.'

Bryn walked down the path, followed by Cadno who barked happily. He thought about the last words of Selwyn, then stopped and shouted at the old man.

'Selwyn, what is the welsh for "Great Dragon"?'

'Y Ddraig Fawr.'

'Say it in English.'

'Try saying 'er thraig vour".'

'Thanks,' said Bryn, and wandered down the path, stumbling over the words, which he repeated over and over.

CHAPTER FOURTEEN

Bryn waited until his mother had taken the last of the lunch plates to the kitchen, then stood in front of his grandfather. Gareth was sitting in his favourite chair, his head hidden by the open Sunday newspaper.

'Granddad, can I have a word, please?'

'Of course, Bryn,' smiled Gareth, and eased the newspaper down on to his lap. 'What can I do for you?'

'First of all, thanks for calming mum down when I got back late for lunch.'

'That's what friends do for each other, isn't it?' said Gareth. 'What else?'

'I've been thinking about this weird man, Emrys Morgan, and would like to find out more about him.'

'Why?'

'Dunno. Suppose it's 'cos him having his grave away from everyone else, for one thing. And if he was so important round here, why don't people want to talk about him?' Bryn scanned his grandfather's face closely, but the bright eyes gave nothing away.

'I told you all I know about him, and people round here do not want to discuss him.'

'Why?'

'He was a very secretive man, for one thing, and…'

'And?'

'He was very powerful round here. People were frightened of him. There are stories about him casting spells on those who upset him. Stories about him being able to conjure up demons, storms, even able to change from human form to animal.' Gareth sighed. 'That is why I don't like talking about that man. He was evil.'

'What sort of animal?'

'It's said he could become a fox,' said Gareth. 'Maybe that's why he was also known as Cadno Du, the 'black fox."

'What do you think?'

'Sounds ridiculous, Bryn, but there are many living here who believe everything. Anything else?'

'Well, for one thing, was he married? Did he have any little Morgans? And if so, what happened to them. No one's said anything about that, or if they were with him when his house was burnt down.'

Gareth stared at his newspaper for a moment. 'I'm not sure why you should be interested, but it so happens that I'm meeting Reverend Lloyd in about an hour. Why not come along, because he might have something in the church records to answer your questions. I believe there was a wife, but as to any children, I have no idea.' Gareth folded his newspaper carefully. 'He will be pleased to see you, because he asked me why you did not come to the service this morning.'

'What did you say?'

'Told a little white lie,' chuckled, Gareth. 'Said you'd joined a football club and were training. Well, you will be next week, so it wasn't much of a lie.'

'Do you believe everything in the bible?'

'I'm not sure what you mean.'

'That "Revelation" bit for a start. All that talk about

beasts, horses, seven seals. Bit frightening, isn't it? I mean no one surely really thinks those terrible things could really happen?'

'There's more things twixt heaven and earth,' Gareth shook his head. 'Can't remember the rest. But I think it means that we must not think everything is black and white.'

'Black and white,' repeated Bryn quietly, then climbed the stairs to his room, thinking about what had just been said.

I do wish grown-ups would not try and be so clever. What the heck was granddad talking about? Bit frightening, that bit about Emrys Morgan being called a black fox, 'cos he could become one. Better get this all down before I forget.

He pulled out his secret notebook and quickly read the two columns, which were rapidly filling with his notes. So much had happened since he began writing, and so much still to learn.

Bryn sucked on a pencil, brow furrowed in concentration, then looked up as Cadno pushed open the door and walked in.

'I wish you could talk,' cos you seem to notice things when we're out,' said Bryn, then hugged his dog who thumped his tail furiously on the floor, and washed his master's hand.

Bryn gently pushed Cadno away, then began writing under the column headed 'What Do I Know'

'1. Selwyn is amazing. His cottage is amazing, and he can do magic. He thinks something, or someone has sent him here to find and stop… what? And who has sent him, 'cos he doesn't even say he thinks there's a God? But he reckons this Emrys Morgan is evil. Sort of a devil, 'cos he can do spells and things. No wonder people here don't want to talk about him. They are frightened of what he can do to them.'

Bryn quickly read the few lines, then crossed out some words.

'I've written about this Morgan guy as though he's still

alive. Emrys was evil, and could do things,' he mumbled, then continued writing. He poured out his thoughts and worries onto the page. So much had happened, and he was sure more was to come. He shivered as he remembered his dreams and the scary events at the stone on Court of Foxes.

'I've got something to do with all this, Cadno. Selwyn knows it, but I wish I knew.' He stroked his dog's head and closed his notebook. 'But then again, maybe I'm glad I don't.'

'Ready in five minutes?' yelled Gareth from the bottom of the stairs.

'Okay, Granddad,' said Bryn, and pushed his notebook back under the mattress.

Bitter cold suddenly filled the room, and the sunlight pouring through the window, was red. Bryn gripped the bedspread from his kneeling position on the floor. Fear flooded over him, leaving him trembling and terrified of something unknown yet obviously evil. Cadno whined, and hurtled out.

A waft of air brushed the nape of his neck as though someone, or something was behind him.

'You are right to think of me as still alive, Bryn,' chuckled a voice in his ear. It was soft, yet vibrant with menace. 'The time is fast approaching when my power will return here, and the prophecy, foretelling of the real Master of the Universe, will come true. You do not yet know why you are a chosen one, but you will.'

The sun became yellow again, the room warm, and Bryn bit his knuckles to stop himself screaming aloud. The voice, so low and quiet, had not only been frightening, but... familiar.

'Waiting, young man,' said Gareth, outside his door, breaking the spell.

They passed through the weathered lychgate, with its

heavily carved wooden canopy, and crunched up the path towards the huge wooden doors of the church. Reverend Broderick Lloyd was waiting for them, a beaming smile of welcome on his face.

'Your grandfather told me you could not listen to God's word this morning, because you might be the next George Best. Ah well, I'm sure the good Lord will understand you exchanging football practice for prayer.'

Bryn nodded, glanced at his impassive faced grandfather, then quickly looked away, stifling the laughter that bubbled inside him. He followed the adults inside the church, and glanced to his right. Two figures were kneeling by the grave of Emrys Morgan, their backs towards him.

'Bryn has some questions for you,' said Gareth, his voice echoing in the high vaulted ceiling.

'Really?' said the vicar, leading them to his office. He shut the door behind them, and motioned his visitors to sit down in the chairs near his desk. Settling himself behind his desk, the vicar leaned back in his chair, and smiled at Bryn.

'And how can I help you?'

'Why don't you like Selwyn? In fact, why doesn't anyone…'

'That's not what you told me you wanted to know,' exploded Gareth, and apologised to Broderick.

'No, he's entitled to an answer,' said the vicar, waving a hand. He stared at Bryn for a moment. 'Selwyn is a bad influence here, and people are frightened of him.'

'Why?' said Bryn. 'He doesn't frighten me.'

'Do you believe in God?'

'Not sure. Been asked that before.'

'Let me put it another way. Do you believe in "Good" and "Evil"?'

'You mean Angels, demons and all that rubbish? Like all that stuff Miss Hughes read last week about the book of

Revelation. She went on a bit, didn't she?'

The vicar sighed. 'Yes, I have to admit, she did "go on a bit" as you said. However, I believe that just as I am a follower of the power of the almighty, there are others who follow the power of darkness.'

'Are you saying that Selwyn is a sort of vicar for Satan?'

'Yes.'

'That's absolute crap,' said Bryn, his voice trembling with emotion.

'Bryn!' snapped Gareth. 'You will apologise at once for such profanities in God's house.'

'Pro, what?' Bryn flushed and looked up at the vicar. 'Sorry, but Selwyn is not bad.' He clenched his fists, and slowly said, 'I know,' staring at the thunder in his grandfather's eyes, and the shock in the vicar's. The atmosphere in the office was electric.

Broderick coughed, then forced a smile. 'And what else was on your mind, Bryn?'

'Emrys Morgan.'

'Oh dear, oh dear,' said the vicar. 'You do take an interest in some unsavoury characters. Now there was someone who wielded power in these parts.'

'Why is he buried away from the other graves?'

'He was, as I said, a very important and powerful man in his time.'

'Maybe,' said Bryn. 'I would have thought he would have had the biggest and best stone on his grave, to show how important he was. But it doesn't explain why he's not buried with the others.'

Broderick looked at Gareth, and contemplated his steepled hands for a moment. 'Truth is, Bryn, that he also indulged in the black arts as well as being a churchgoer. In fact he used his wealth to help repair this church. He also paid for a beautiful stained glass window. However, the elders of the church did not want his final resting place to be on hallowed ground. They clashed with those who were his followers. So a compromise was reached as Emrys had a plot, paid for during his lifetime. When he died, the vicar at the time consecrated the plot where he now lies, so everyone was satisfied.'

'So who looks after his grave? You?'

'No, Bryn, but there are still those who live in Morredin who think he was someone very special.'

'Like those two I saw as we came in?'

'Probably.' The vicar shuffled some papers on his desk, and Bryn realised he did not want to continue talking about Emrys Morgan.

'Was he married?'

'I believe so,' said the vicar. 'In fact, I know so, and if you come with me, we can check the Parish records.' He led the way out of the office to a small room behind the altar. 'Why do you want to know?'

'Dunno.'

I really don't know, thought Bryn. But something tells me I must find out all there is to know about Emrys Morgan. I'm involved in some strange way. Selwyn knew the very first time we met. He told me he thought I was here for a purpose. Trouble is I haven't a clue what it is.

He watched the vicar go to a bookshelf, peer through his spectacles at the line of leather-bound volumes, and pull one out.

'If my memory serves me correctly, it will be in this one.' He took the book to a table, and quickly flicked through the pages. The vicar stopped, scanned the writing, and turned back one page. His head nodded, and he took off his spectacles and tapped the page.

'Here it is, young man. Come and read for yourself.'

Bryn slowly read the detail of Emrys Morgan's wedding.

The simple inscription recorded his marriage with Alice Morris, 'Spinster'. They were married in December 1833 at the village church, 'with consent of parents,' by Licence.

'What is a "spinster"?'

'It means the young lady had never been married before.'

'So how old was he when he got married?'

'Let me see,' said the vicar. 'I believe he was born in 1787, so…' he mumbled to himself, eyes shut to help his concentration. 'Ah, now I have it. It would have made him about forty six.'

'Was his wife with him when his place burnt down?'

The vicar coughed, and closed the book. He replaced it in the bookshelf, then turned round and slowly wiped his spectacles before placing them in their case.

'No, Bryn. In fact she had left her husband a few years previously.'

'Why?'

'There are many stories and rumours. Some say he beat her, others that he cavorted with other young ladies, and there are other, more frightening stories.'

'What sort of stories?'

'It is said that she witnessed him calling up demons, and was so terrified one night, her brown hair was white by morning.'

'What happened to her?'

'Not sure, Bryn. I know she left Morredin, taking her young son with her.'

Bryn felt a strange tingle run down his spine at the information. His head was bursting with so many thoughts about Emrys, foxes, secret caves.

'Where did they go?'

'Who knows?' sighed, Broderick. 'From all accounts, when Emrys came home from one of his trips, his wife and child were gone. As though they had vanished into thin air. She was born here, and there is no record of family anywhere else.'

'I suppose she would have eventually heard of his death,' said Gareth. 'Was there a will?'

'None that I know of,' said the vicar. 'Pity, because he was a wealthy man and we could use some of that now.' Broderick led them out of the room into the church aisle. He pointed up to the roof. 'That needs some urgent repairs.'

He walked to the front of the church, and stopped by a brightly coloured window set in the wall.

'This is the window Emrys had made.'

Bryn stared at the colours, vivid as the sun made the scene dance as though alive. He could see a vixen playing with her cubs round the altar stone on the hill. A vague figure stood in the background, silhouetted against the blue sky. Arms outstretched, the viewer could imagine him to be a Saint or, Satan.

As they walked out of the church, Bryn touched the vicar's arm, as he was deep in conversation with his grandfather.

'Yes, Bryn.'

'Where did Emrys come from?'

'That is one of the mysteries, as he wasn't a Morredin man. When he came, he was already a wealthy man. Certainly he gave work to many here on his farm, and the extensions he built on Plas Cadno. As to why he married poor Alice Morris, there is another mystery. Probably, to have an heir.'

'But an heir to what?' muttered Gareth.

'Indeed,' said the vicar. He looked at his watch. 'Good heavens, how time flies, and we haven't even talked about why you're here, Gareth.'

'You go home, Bryn, and I'll stay and conclude my business with the vicar.'

Bryn wandered out of the church, and saw the couple still

by the grave of the strange Emrys Morgan. They appeared to have finished their work and turned as he walked over the grass towards them.

Carys smiled as she picked up a bunch of dead flowers and place them in an old supermarket bag. She watched Bryn walk over and stare at the grave. The grass had been tidied with a pair of shears that Gwyn still held. Fresh flowers stood in an urn on the white pebbles on the surface of the last resting place of Emrys.

'You've done a good job,' said Bryn.

'Thank you,' said Carys.

'Relative of yours?'

'No.'

'Then why bother?'

'Someone has to.'

'Really?' said Bryn, and turned round. 'Then what about that lot over there? There's loads of graves need more attention than this one'

'You wouldn't understand, Bryn, not being born here.'

'Try me.' Bryn, anger rising, wanted some answers.

'This is the grave of a very important man, who still means a lot to Morredin.'

'I've seen his window in the church. Liked foxes, didn't he?' Bryn traced the shape of the headstone with a hand. 'In fact foxes are, or I should say, "were" very important here.'

Carys bit her lip, and stared at Bryn, then at Gwyn, who shrugged his shoulders. She tossed her hair, as though coming to a decision.

'Maybe, now you live here, you should meet the others.'

'Others?'

'I'm saying no more. If you want to learn, then be at the school at ten tonight.'

'Mum won't let me go out, that time of night.'

Carys pulled a face. 'That's your problem, Bryn. Ten

tonight, and we'll give you five minutes, no more.'

She picked up the bag, and walked past Bryn, followed by a silent Gwyn, carrying the shears.

CHAPTER FIFTEEN

Bryn pulled his bobble hat down over his ears. The rising wind was very cold, and he thrust his hands deep inside the pockets of his anorak. There was a nip of frost in the air. He shuffled along the street, ignoring the stares from the few adults who passed.

I must be mad coming out this time of night, he thought. But I want to find out what they do in that cave. Wonder what made Carys invite me? Gwyn didn't seem very happy. Mum was surprised when I said I had a headache and went to bed at nine.

He smiled as he remembered lying with his eyes closed, and breathing deeply when his mother crept into his bedroom. She had stroked his hair, then gently kissed his cheek before leaving and closing his door carefully.

He had waited a few minutes, then crept put of bed. Taking off his pyjama jacket revealed him fully clothed. It had been easy to pull on his trainers and a thick jumper. He grabbed his anorak which he had secreted up to his room, then opened his bedroom window.

Easing out onto the ledge, he was able to grasp the thick branch of a tree overhanging the roof. Quickly shimming down the trunk, Bryn crouched down by the side of the cottage, as Cadno, hearing him, barked a warning.

'Cadno, be quiet,' cried Gareth. 'There's no one there.'

Bryn heard the front door open, and the light streamed out as his grandfather peered round then closed the door. The barking ceased, and Bryn inched his way out of the garden.

As he reached the school, several figures detached themselves from the gloom and walked towards him. He recognised Carys and Gwyn, and two more classmates.

'Any trouble?' said Carys.

'Mum still thinks I'm fast asleep.' Bryn looked round. 'Anyone else coming?'

'Some will join us as we go to the place.'

'What place?'

'You'll have to be patient, Bryn,' said Carys. 'You will learn a lot, and understand more.' She turned and led the group along the street and out of the village. Only the sound of shuffling feet broke the silence apart from the moaning of the wind and the rustle of the trees.

A half moon gave some light, and Bryn noticed the group walked confidently along the path by the side of the stream. The bubbling waters shimmered, and he was not surprised when Carys turned off the path and began climbing the hill.

Two more children were waiting at the junction. Nothing was said, nor recognition given as they joined the group. Bryn found the silence oppressive, and felt increasingly worried as they climbed.

What had begun as a bit of fun, and a desire to find out what happened in the cave, was now disturbing. Detective Bryn was no longer feeling confident. If anything, he was becoming frightened, and beginning to wish he hadn't come.

Carys and Gwyn switched on torches and pointed out the

track up the hillside. Bryn looked from side to side, expecting to see pairs of eyes from following foxes. His imagination saw the creatures loping along in the darkness, their lithe forms close to the ground.

A cry as someone stumbled over a rock, whispered 'shush' from the others, and the group continued on their journey. Bryn looked at the back of Carys's head and wondered what she was thinking. He was aware of an increasing excitement as they reached the top and stopped for a moment to look down at the plateau below.

The wind increased in intensity. Bryn shivered, not with cold, but mounting fear. His eyes were drawn to the far side as a flash of lightning bathed the slope in eerie light. Distant thunder echoed in the hills.

Outlined against the night sky stood a figure. It was motionless, but appeared to be clothed in a hooded gown, with the face hidden. When another zigzag of brilliant light hissed out of the sky, the figure had vanished.

'Dyn Hysbys,' whispered Carys 'He watches.'

Could have been Selwyn, thought Bryn, as the group slowly made their way down the slope. He followed at the back as Carys led them along the path to the opening of the cave. The torchlight helped them pick their way over the stones and rubble until they stood at the entrance.

'Do not say anything or ask questions,' said Carys, laying a hand on Bryn's arm. 'Just look, listen and learn. Okay?'

Bryn nodded, and watched her walk inside the entrance. He heard the scrape of a match being struck, then she appeared holding a flickering candle. Only the shuffling of feet entering the cave disturbed the brooding silence. The other candles were lit, and dancing shadows bounced off the walls giving the impression that they were not alone.

I wonder when she last went to the cave, thought Bryn. 'cos she must have been surprised to see the candle used up. She must have known someone else has been here. Wonder if she suspects me, and that's why I've been invited? Must be on my guard, and not give her any reason to think I've been here.

The two black candles on the altar stone were burning well, as Carys walked forwards. She stood for a moment staring at the wall opposite, then knelt down, muttering some strange words that Bryn could scarcely hear. He looked at his companions, but all eyes were on Carys.

Slowly she rose, carrying the box, which Bryn had found, then turned to face the group. She nodded to Gwyn who walked forwards, and reached inside the cleft in the wall for the key.

'Adentium, mesantium,' she said in a flat voice, as the padlock clicked on opening. Carys held the box until Gwyn had taken the old book and laid it on the altar, then closed the lid, and placed it on the ground at her feet.

She turned round to face the others. Her eyes were wild in the flickering candlelight, and she trembled with excitement. Holding out the book, she spoke softly.

'This is the book of truths, written by the "Wise One." Only he knows the secrets of its pages. But we gather here, his followers, to read and hope for eternal knowledge.'

'Give us your knowledge, "Wise One", we beseech you,' mumbled the other children in unison. They held out their arms, and slowly walked toward the book. Each, in turn, placed their hands, palms downwards, on the open pages and bent their heads. They then kissed the book and returned to their places.

'What about you, Bryn?' said Carys, and everyone turned to look at him.

'What is that book?'

'The Book of Knowledge.'

'About what?'

'About everything,' whispered Carys. 'Dyn Hysbys knew everything about life and death.'

'And it's all in that book?' Bryn stared at Carys, trying to think logically. If his dreams had something to do with the weird events at Morredin, then this was not the book. Selwyn believes that there is truth in that Revelation stuff. And if he's right, then the special book has seven locks. This one hasn't any. No, this is not the special book.

'So who's this "Wise One"?' Bryn knew the answer, but wanted to hear it from Carys.

'You will find out, when we think you are ready.'

'Rubbish,' said Bryn, and heard the sharp intake of breath from Gwyn. 'I already know. It's that weirdo, whose grave you look after. Emrys Morgan, isn't it?'

He looked round and saw the worry in several faces. Carys said nothing, but walked towards him, still holding the open book.

'Are you prepared to learn?'

Bryn felt the atmosphere close round him, stifling, crushing, and there was something else. He sensed a presence behind him, cold air once again wafting the nape of his neck. When he felt the pressure of a hand gently squeeze his right shoulder, Bryn wanted to scream out.

'Well?' said Carys, her voice demanding an answer.

Bryn was terrified. He wanted to look round, but dare not, scared of what–or who, he might see. The other children were watching him, their eyes bright with excitement and anticipation. It was as if they had been taken over by some powerful force that made them robots under the spell and command of, who?

'I don't want to join,' cried Bryn, and pushing past Gwyn, fled from the cave, past the flickering candle in the entrance and out into a pitch black night. The moon was just hiding behind a scudding cloud as he began to scramble up the slope.

Behind him the children were chanting something, and their voices were raised, louder and louder as the magic in the cave took control.

Bryn clawed his way up the rubble, crying with fear. This was no longer a game, but something else. Maybe there really was an evil power in the village, which had taken control of the group in the cave. Carys and the others had sounded different, looked different. I bet they'll be their usual selves in school tomorrow, and not even talk about tonight. Just want to get home, back to bed. Should never have come out. It's so cold out here.

He finally scrambled to the top, then ran across the plateau, barely able to make out the path as the moon appeared again. His feet crunched through the freezing grass, his chest aching with the exertion of running and breathing bitterly cold air. He turned to run up the slope, and stubbed a toe on a rocky outcrop. His twisting body thudded down. Bryn lay on the grass, gulping in air. The stillness of the night was menacing, and yet his ears picked up a sound that seemed to come from the other side of the plateau.

He sat up and turned to stare at the slope where the hooded figure had appeared, and his heart hurtled against his chest. The sky over the slope was red, as though a fire raged out of control. On the ridge, outlined in the red glow, were six dog-like shapes, silently looking in his direction

'They're not there. I'm seeing things. No one else sees foxes 'cept me. If I blink my eyes, they'll go away,' whispered Bryn. He closed his eyes, then squinted at the distant slope. The foxes were still there, and now moving down towards the plateau. Their lithe forms glided over the ground, effortlessly, silently. As one, they stopped, stared in his direction, then gathered pace and ran across the ground. Another six appeared on the slope, hesitated a moment, then followed their companions.

Bryn turned and using hands and feet scrambled and clawed his way up the slope, sobbing quietly. He had no idea why the foxes had appeared, but was conscious that he was the target of their rush.

Reaching the top, he gulped the air, and screamed when he saw a hooded figure standing motionless. He collapsed on the grass, and curled into a tight ball.

'What is it that troubles you? And why are you out at this time of night, Bryn, in this cold?'

'Selwyn?' whispered Bryn, peering up from his crouched position.

'Who else?' said Selwyn, and reached down to help Bryn.

'It's those foxes coming over here. Hundreds of them.'

'What foxes, Bryn? I see no foxes.'

'There,' said Bryn, slowly getting to his feet and pointing at the distant hillock, brightly illuminated in the blood red sky. He stared at the slope and the plateau below, but there was nothing. No slinking foxes running towards them.

'But they were there,' whispered Bryn, and turned towards the distant cave. The low voices of the children were louder as they left the cave, climbed to the top of the entrance, then stood in a line.

Only the flickering glow from the candles they held betrayed their presence, as they intoned prayers from a belief alien to Bryn.

'Let us not stay here, my young friend,' said Selwyn. 'You have intruded into something you were ill advised, and might regret. Your curiosity into investigating the unknown is taking you into dangerous waters.'

They walked away from the plateau and the strange cave, only the low thud of Selwyn's staff hitting the ground disturbing the silence. Bryn found himself trotting to keep up with the old man, striding down the path.

'We must get you home before your mother is aware you

no longer occupy your bed.'

'Why, yet again, was I the only one to see foxes, 'cos they were there, Selwyn. I'm not seeing things.'

'I have been ruminating for a long time on that phenomenon, and believe even more passionately you are here for a purpose.'

'Rummy what?'

'Thinking. I've been thinking.'

'Wish you'd speak English to me, Selwyn.'

'Could be worse,' smiled the old man. 'I might only be able to speak Welsh.'

'Do you think Carys will say anything tomorrow at school?'

'It is my belief she, and the others, will pursue the day as though nothing untoward happened this night. And I would suggest you go along with that.'

They finally reached the path alongside the stream, and Selwyn stopped. 'I will leave you now, Bryn, and let you go home. I hope you can gain your room with the same ease as you left, and not disturb anyone.'

'So do I. Mum would kill me if she knew I was out.' Bryn looked at the glistening water. 'Why were you out so late?'

'I find the silence of the night a good time to walk and think. It focuses the mind, and there is much that has happened since you arrived at Morredin. So I'll say, goodnight and hope you can get some sleep before the morning's endeavours.'

'Night then, Selwyn. See you soon?'

'Oh yes, my young friend. Of that be assured.'

Bryn began to trot down the path, then stopped as a sudden thought struck him.

'Selwyn?' he cried, turning to face the old man.

'What troubles you now?'

'It was you on the other slope who saw us go into the cave, wasn't it?'

'No, Bryn. What a strange question,' said Selwyn. He waved, and strode quickly away.

CHAPTER SIXTEEN

Bryn was grinning to himself as he walked to school the next morning. He yawned as the lack of sleep hit him, but he was in a good mood. Climbing back up the tree to his room had been easy, and even Cadno had not been disturbed. The only problem had been falling into a deep sleep as soon as his head hit the pillow. Waking was difficult.

'Bryn, will you wake up!' shouted his mother. 'I called you ages ago. If you don't get a move on, you're going to be late for school.'

'Sorry, Mum,' mumbled Bryn. 'Didn't sleep well.'

'Bad dreams again?'

'Sort of.'

'Maybe we ought to see someone about those dreams. Maybe you need a tonic or something.'

'Don't fuss, Mum, I'm okay,' said Bryn, noting, with satisfaction, the concern in her voice.

Bryn thought about the previous night's events, especially Selwyn's insistence he had not been the person watching them all troupe into the cave. If it wasn't Selwyn, then who was it? Don't believe Carys saying it was that Morgan

149

character. He's dead, and I don't believe in ghosts.

'Or do I?' said Bryn aloud as he remembered the ghostly hand on his shoulder in the cave. It had felt so real, that firm squeeze. 'Would there really have been someone if I'd turned round?'

'Talking to yourself again, I see,' said Carys, running up to him.

'Just thinking.'

'Do anything interesting after I saw you in the churchyard?'

'I…' mumbled Bryn, then remembered what Selwyn had told him. Carys was pretending nothing happened the previous night. Okay, two can play at that game.

'Nothing much, except for one thing.'

'What's that?'

'Heard the foxes in the hills again. Must have been loads of them barking.'

'But there aren't any foxes here now. You know that.' said Carys, then waved to another girl and ran away to greet her in Welsh.

As he turned into the road leading to school, he saw Gwyn ahead and ran up to him.

'Did you stay long after I left last night?'

'What do you mean?' stammered Gwyn, and tried to stride ahead, but was stopped by Bryn's hand on his arm.

'The cave. Don't try and tell me you've forgotten.'

'Rather not talk about it.' Gwyn stopped, and shrugged Bryn's hand off. 'And if you've any sense, you'll not tell anybody what you saw.' He ran away to catch up with Carys and her friends. They turned round, stared at Bryn for a moment, then continued walking.

So they want to keep their secret, thought Bryn. Stupid anyway, Carys talking all that rubbish in the cave. Anyway, I know that's not the book, and I know there's another, special, cave somewhere. But it is odd, inviting me to go last night. After all, I wasn't even born here, thank goodness. Wonder what they were hoping I'd do…or say? Wish I was back in Derby, playing for the Rams. Wish they were doing better.

'Bore da, Bryn,' wheezed Hugh Price, and dismounted from his cycle. 'You seem deep in thought, young man.'

'Morning, sir,' said Bryn, then came to a decision. 'Can I talk you about something?'

'Of course. I'm all ears.'

Yes you are, thought Bryn, staring at the large protruding appendages on each side of the teacher's head. He bit his lip to stop himself chuckling.

'What do you know about the caves round here?'

'There are a lot of them, Bryn. Hills are riddled with 'em. And we must not forget the gold mines which are also reached through caves.'

'But have you heard of a special cave?'

'Special? What is so special about this "special" cave?'

Bryn looked at the large round eyes of the teacher, one eyebrow raised quizzically. There was no expression in the gaze, no surprise, no interest.

'Nothing really. Just something I'd heard in the village.'

'What, exactly, did you hear?'

'Just that one is used for meetings, or something. Just a rumour, I suppose, if you've never heard of it.'

Hugh mounted his cycle again, and grasped the handlebars firmly. As he pushed one foot down on the pedal to move away, he smiled at Bryn.

'No I haven't, but have heard you are pretty good at soccer from Bob Holbrook.'

'Then you will also have heard how I missed a sitter the other day.'

'Heard something like that. Anyway, I've decided that this afternoon, during sports period, we'll try soccer.' Hugh smiled. 'Give you a chance to show how good you really are.' With a final wave, the teacher slowly pedalled away. Bryn punched the air, and shouted, 'Yes!' which caused other bemused children to turn round and stare.

Bryn ran out of the school onto the playing field, and looked at the goal post leaning drunkenly to one side. He knew that the preferred game at Morredin was rugby, and had tried to get interested. Running with a ball, trying to evade your opponent was stupid compared to the thrill of soccer. One neat feint on the run, sending the other footballer sliding in the wrong direction, was magic.

He watched Hugh Price waddle out of the school with four footballs tucked under his arms. Reaching the centre of the pitch, a shrill blast from the whistle in his mouth made the children stop talking.

'What's he got footballs for?' said Gwyn.

'Can't play rugby with those,' said Carys, scraping her hair behind her head tying it with a thick elastic band.

'Right, children,' said Hugh, dropping the footballs. 'Today, we will compare the game of soccer with the real game.'

'Why?' grumbled Carys.

'For one thing, Carys. You are not allowed to bring your opponent to the ground. Now I know that will be a disappointment to you,' said Hugh, and joined the chuckles of the others. 'In Bryn's game, in which I have heard he has quite a talent, you can only use your football skills.'

Bryn watched the teacher, dressed in tight jeans and a rugby shirt, kick one of the footballs ahead, then beckon to him.

'Now Bryn will show us how to take the ball off your opponent, only using your feet. Watch carefully, Carys, and you will learn something.'

Bryn reddened, aware that all the children were watching him. It was going to be easy getting the ball away from the overweight teacher. No real test. Not proving anything.

'Ready, Bryn?'

'Yes, Sir,' said Bryn and trotted towards Hugh who lumbered towards him.

Encouraged by the shouts of his watching classmates, Bryn stuck out a foot to dispossess Hugh, but only struck grass. The ball was neatly flicked between his legs, and Bryn could only stop and look into the grinning face of the teacher.

'Shall we try again?'

That was a fluke, thought Bryn. You can't play football. You're too fat anyway. I'll show you next time. He nodded, and waited until Hugh began to amble towards him, then trotted to intercept, eyes fixed on the football.

When Hugh leaned to his right, Bryn grinned. He had met that feint many times in matches, and waited for the ball to pass across, except it didn't. As he eased to the opposite side, the teacher flicked the ball over his head, and lumbered past to kick the ball down the field. The teacher stopped, pulled a handkerchief from his head, and mopped his sweaty face.

'Your turn now, Bryn. Take the ball and get it past me.'

'Right, Sir,' said Bryn, and ran across to intercept the football as it rolled towards him, his mind in turmoil. This is silly. Farty Hughes is making a complete idiot of me. I'll show him now it's my turn. I'll have him sliding all over the field.

Bryn kicked the ball ahead and began to run, tapping the ball, keeping it just in front of himself. The teacher swayed, then danced from foot to foot, watching the advancing Bryn, who weaved from side to side.

As he approached Hugh, Bryn juggled the ball from one foot to the other, feinted to his right, then spun on his foot and shot clear of the teacher. His grin of triumph vanished as he heard Hugh cry, 'I think you've forgotten something.'

Bryn stopped, turned round and saw the teacher standing with one foot on the ball. The children were laughing, jumping up and down, and clapping their hands.

'How did you do that?'

'Ah, Bryn, there are some things you never forget, like riding a bike.'

'But I was told you were good at rugby, sir.'

'True, but in my younger days, I also played football on occasion. Not too bad either.' He tapped his portly frame. 'Hard to believe, I know.'

Bryn looked at the teacher, and felt new respect. Anyone who could control a football with such dexterity was someone special. It was hard to imagine this blubbery figure had once been a fit sportsman in his youth.

'Right, children,' said Hugh, picking up the ball. 'Get yourselves into two teams, and we will try ball control.' He glared at the glum faces. 'It can be fun, and will also be useful for rugby.'

Bryn watched the two lines and Hugh placing a ball at the feet of the first person. He had decided to be at the back of his line, headed by Gwyn. This was an exercise he knew well. The difference being that he had been used to having to dribble the ball in an out of a line of small cones. Here, the children would just run forwards in pairs to Hugh, tapping the ball back and forth to each other they progressed up the field.

He casually glanced up towards the two peaks of the 'Court of Foxes,' and stared. The sun appeared to be behind the black crags, and had changed colour to a blood red. Reddish billowing clouds gave the impression the whole of the range was on fire. It looked as if tongues of flame were licking the summit. Weird, wonderful, and, Bryn shivered at the thought, frightening. Of course the hill is not on fire, not really. Just looks like it, but those flames do look real. What does it mean?

'Bryn, it's your turn,' shouted the teacher. 'Wake up, boy. The others want to see how good you are.'

'Sorry,' mumbled Bryn, seeing the ball by his feet, and the last boy in the other line watching him closely.

He glanced at the distant fiery hills, then trotted forward, gathering pace as he kicked the ball across to his right. His companion missed connecting with the ball, and Bryn mumbled under his breath, and waited for the ball to be retrieved.

Slowly, they reached the teacher then Bryn, having the ball at his feet, rounded Hugh Price, and raced back to the other children then stopped. He kicked the ball into the air, then stood still, using his head to keep it airborne, basking in the cheers, jeers, and clapping of his classmates.

'That's not what I had in mind to finish the run,' sighed Hugh, 'but I wouldn't want to stop your fun.'

Then the rain came, slowly at first, with an increasing wind, which ruffled the grass, and made surrounding trees sway to its power.

'I think we are in for a downpour, children,' said Hugh, bending down to pick up a football. 'Get back to the school, as quick as you can.'

Bryn grabbed another two balls, and saw Carys pick up the fourth, then stand with Gwyn and stare at the hills. This is not right, he thought. Something's very odd, and Carys knows. This wind's getting stronger, and so is the rain… or is it rain now?

He flinched, his face stung by hard, icy missiles. Some of the children screamed as they stampeded out of the field. A carpet of white rapidly covered the grass. He began to run, hunching his shoulders against the deluge hurtling down from the blood red sky. It was the same colour he had seen before.

The missiles were hurting now as they increased in size. Over it all, the brooding peaks of the mysterious hill stood sentinel to the mayhem below, as thunder rumbled ominously overhead.

Bryn reached the side door into the school, hearing the drumming of thousands of hailstones on the roof. He looked round and saw the soaking children standing quietly or whimpering softly. Everyone was frightened at the sudden change from sunny afternoon to the avalanche from the sky.

Bryn wiped his wet hair from his eyes, and walked to a window. The deluge was easing, then as suddenly as it came, the hail ceased, and the ground was bathed in sunlight. It's just like that time when I was at Selwyn's, 'cept this is worse. It's a message, or warning, from someone,… or something.

'Don't stand there too long, Bryn,' said Hugh, standing by his side. 'Get yourself towelled down, and change out of that wet kit.'

'Has it ever done that before, Sir?'

'Sudden hail, you mean?' Hugh rubbed his hair with a large towel. 'Not unusual in these parts, but the size of these hailstones is something else. Never seen hail as big as this.' He opened the door, stooped, and picked up a handful of the white balls. 'Look at these? Must be size of golf balls. Wouldn't be surprised if there's a lot of damage in the village.'

Mobile phones were ringing as worried parents contacted their children, and Bryn listened to the conversations, mostly in Welsh. His mother could not afford such a luxury for him, though he had argued that all his classmates had one. He knew that wasn't true, but it enforced his argument.

'Want to let your mother know you are safe?' said Hugh, handing out his telephone.

'Thanks, sir. Mum is out at work, but Granddad will be worried. Just give him a quick call.' He watched the teacher nod, then walk away, before dialling the cottage.

'All right, son?' said a worried grandfather. 'Been awful here. All the glass in my greenhouse is smashed. Heard that Mrs Benson, from down the road, opened her door when the hail came, and got hit in the face by dozens of 'em. Gave her two black eyes.'

Bryn grinned. He visualised the overweight woman from down the road, with the loud voice and bad temper. Couldn't happen to a nicer person.

'Poor Mrs Benson,' he said, trying to show concern, then rang off after assuring his grandfather no one had been hurt. He walked to the teacher and returned the mobile phone, then wandered into the changing rooms.

As he stripped himself, and dried his body, Bryn thought about the sudden ending of the sports afternoon. It was confusing, yet he had the gut feeling there had been a reason for that sudden, impossible, weather change. It all seemed connected with that 'Revelation' stuff, and he would read more about it. Selwyn knew a lot, so he would go and see him soon.

Leaving the school, Bryn could see teachers in shock, looking at the dimpled appearance of the roofs of their cars. A few had broken windows. The hail still lay heaped in piles in the shade, but was rapidly melting where the sun's rays shone strongly down again.

Bryn walked past flattened plants, and could see sheep huddled together for protection and comfort. Even though their thick fleece would have given protection, he guessed the ferocity of the hailstones would have been terrifying for the animals.

Carys and her friends had left the school together, not wanting to talk to him. That's okay, thought Bryn. Not the first time she's ignored me when it suits her. I wonder what she thinks about the hail. Does she think it has anything to with what goes on in her cave, or "Diss Hiss", or whatever she calls that guy in the grave? Farty Hugh doesn't seem to think it terribly odd though. Said it's happened before.

As he pushed open the cottage door, Cadno rushed out to greet him, barking his delight.

'Is that you, Bryn?' said Gareth. 'We're on the telly already. Come and look.'

Bryn ambled through to the front room and watched the images on the television. The cameras showed fields covered, inches deep, in the hail. Close up views of dented cars and interviews with their owners, then the cameras showed the shattered greenhouses on a farm.

He was not surprised when the interviewer said that the mystery of the deluge was that only Morredin and the outlying farms had been affected.

'Meteorologists have told me that it is a freak quirk of nature,' said the interviewer.

'Or there might be another explanation, which has nothing to do with nature,' mumbled Bryn.

'What did you say?'

'Nothing, Granddad. Just thinking.'

As he climbed the stairs to write another entry in his secret book, Bryn thought back to the hailstorm in the field. He tried to recall the detail of his visit to Selwyn. Then the hailstones had not been as large, but sudden and unexpected in their appearance none the less. Selwyn had been able to stop the storm by saying some strange words. Bryn tried to remember what seemed a command. Definitely a command from Selwyn, but he could not recall the actual words.

But one memory remained very clear, and it was disturbing. Before he joined the others in the stampede back to the school, Bryn saw his teacher stop and stare at the distant hills. When he turned round, his face showed no sign of worry or fright. A knowing smile bathed his features in tranquillity.

CHAPTER SEVENTEEN

B ryn frowned as he read the words in the bible he had borrowed from his grandfather. Gareth had been surprised at the attention his grandson had given when trying to help him with understanding the Welsh language. Mr Price had enlisted the help of Gareth in the task. Usually, Bryn made his disinterest and lack of concern very obvious.

'It's not as if anyone speaks the stuff except round here,' mumbled Bryn one night, after a particularly hard session. 'It's daft making me, an Englishman, have to learn it. Anyway, it's so crappy hard to speak, and none of the words make any sense.'

Gareth's face crumpled momentarily as he heard the swearing, then tapped the school book. 'It's a beautiful language, Bryn. The words roll gently off the tongue. That is why we Welsh produce such good singers.' He smiled at the boy. 'And for the record, having a Welsh mother, makes you at least half Welsh.'

As he watched his grandson pay more than usual attention, he guessed there would be a request for a favour afterwards. He was not prepared on being asked for a loan of his bible.

Without any explanation, Bryn thanked him, then left the room, with Cadno by his side, and went to his room.

Bryn sat on the edge of his bed, with Cadno's head resting on his feet. The dog looked up at him with bright eyes, and was stroked, resulting in a fierce wagging of his tail.

'Glad you weren't out there. Big as cricket balls, those hailstones,' said Bryn, then placed the bible on his knees and turned the pages. 'Can't play now, must look at this. Maybe it's not all just words, but there's a message in here somewhere.'

As he flicked through the pages of "Revelation", Bryn searched for something, anything, to make sense of the strange events. Selwyn had told him Morredin was the centre of something evil, and clues were to be found in the weird words of the bible.

He took out his secret notebook, and began to make notes, as he read. A definite link was forming between the various sections of "Revelation".

'Lots of hail seem to chucked around,' he said, then stabbed a finger at one passage. It said that huge hailstones, weighing about one hundred pounds each, fell. Another section talked of hail and fire, and he slowly read part of one sentence aloud.

'And something like a huge mountain, all ablaze, was thrown into the sea.' Bryn read it again, and tapped his teeth with the end of his biro, before making notes.

There wasn't a sea, and the hills hadn't really been ablaze, just looked like it, with the sun behind colouring the irregular cloud formation. Still, he thought, it ties in with the hail, and the thunder, which is also in the bible. And what is this Armageddon in Revelation 16? Is Morredin another name for it? Granddad would know.

He wrote furiously under his two headings of 'What do I know' and 'What I must find out,' then closed his book, and replaced it in his hiding place. All this Bible stuff was just a story, wasn't it? But suppose there was some truth written there? Suppose Selwyn really knows something really awful could happen here? Then why am I important? And why is it only me still sees foxes, and hears 'em? And why do I have dreams about blood, horses in the sky, and a mysterious cave?

Cadno brought him out of his reverie by crying softly, and using a paw to tap his leg. Bryn looked down to see his dog sitting up, ears erect and tongue lolling in his mouth.

'Want to play, do you?' said Bryn, and stood up, then opened the door. Cadno hurtled down the stairs, and his master followed.

'Find out what you wanted?' said Gareth, turning round in his chair by the fire.

'Sort of,' said Bryn, then stopped as he reached the front door. 'Granddad, what does 'Armar, something or other, mean?'

'Armageddon, that's the word you mean. It's supposed to be where the final battle between the powers of good and evil will take place.' Gareth laid his newspaper on his lap, and looked up at his grandson. 'Some would say the fight's begun, what with the horrors man has done since the last war. Hardly a day without killings, bombing, so-called ethnic cleansing.' He sighed. 'Maybe we are already seeing Armageddon.'

'Yeah, but that Revelation stuff talks about red horses, white horses, black horses, in the sky and…'

'That's just people writing to frighten the readers,' interrupted Gareth. 'In the old days, centuries ago, everyone was afraid of the men of the cloth. They were powerful people.' He smiled. 'I can still remember trembling with fear on a Sunday in church, when the Minister would preach hell and damnation if we did not repent our sins. And as a boy, always into mischief, I thought I was doomed. Of course, as soon as I was out of church, and playing with my friends again, all thoughts of what would happen to me in the hereafter vanished.'

Bryn grinned at his grandfather, then rushed across to hug him. 'Glad you were a bit like me.'

'Reckon I could have shown you a thing or two, young man. Now be off with you. Cadno's waiting, and judging from his barking, he's getting impatient.'

'Just had a thought. Did you see the sun before it began to rain?'

'I was outside in the garden. Why?'

'What colour was it?'

'It was so bright, I could hardly stare at it.'

'Was it red?'

'No, Bryn, definitely not red. Why do you ask?'

'Nothing, Granddad.'

Bryn waved goodbye, and closed the door behind him. The sky was blue, and his dog bounded ahead as he turned right to reach the main street. Small piles of the icy balls were still visible in the gardens and on the hillside, but Bryn was not thinking about that sudden weather change.

Granddad had said the stories about horses in the sky were not really true. Then how come he had seen them in his nightmare, and that awful, black clad… skeleton?

As he reached the main street, Bryn could see Selwyn emerge from a shop, carrying a bulging plastic bag. He stopped to talk to Bob Holbrook who was passing.

'Come and talk to us, Bryn,' called Selwyn, looking up and hearing Cadno bark at an irate cat, sitting on a wall and spitting its defiance.

'Were you caught out in the hail?' asked Bob.

'Supposed to be doing football with Farty in the playing field when it happened.'

'Bet that made him active,' chuckled Bob, and winked at Bryn.

'Dear, dear,' said Selwyn, waving his hands in mock horror. 'Don't encourage young Bryn to be insubordinate to his teachers.'

'So did Farty, sorry, Mr Price, know anything about football?' said Bob.

'He can still control a football. Looking at him now, I find it hard to imagine him as a rugby player.'

'Talking of football, fancy a game on Saturday morning?'

'You mean, you'll give me another chance?'

'Look, Bryn. We all make mistakes, and I've persuaded the others it was just a blip. I believe you have got talent. Just needs working on.' Bob grinned. 'Let's face it, the Rams could do with some talent these days, the way they've slipped down the table.' He looked at his wristwatch. 'Must be off. I'll pick you up at eight. Kick-off's at half past ten.'

Bryn watched the football coach stride away, then turned to Selwyn. 'What colour was the sun when the rain came?'

'What a surprising question. Just very, very bright, and… why do you ask?'

'Not red then?'

'No, but you haven't answered my question.'

'Well, I saw it go red, and 'cos the moving clouds behind the hill also looked red…'

'And something like a huge mountain, all ablaze, was thrown into the sea.' Selwyn's face was stern. 'Revelation Eight.'

'Yeah, it looked like flames were coming out from the top of the Court of Foxes. Thing is, only I seem to have seen the sun go red.' Bryn clutched the sleeve of Selwyn's jacket. 'What does it mean? Why am I seeing things no one else does?'

'I am not sure, but several thoughts have permeated my mind over the past few days. Something is about to happen that will be momentous, and I fear dangerous. Of more importance, I believe it will affect you.' He stared at Bryn, then grasped his staff firmly. 'I want to show you something, that no one in this village has seen.'

'What is it?'

'I will not divulge anything. It is important you have no idea until you see for yourself.' Selwyn glanced across the road to see a group of children staring at him. 'I see Carys and her friends are taking an interest in us.' He placed a hand on Bryn's shoulder. 'I will meet you at the stepping stones in an hour. In the meantime, say nothing about this conversation to anybody.'

Bryn watched him stride quickly away, then watched Carys and the others walk across to join him.

'What did he want?' demanded Carys.

'Nothing, he was talking to me and Mr Holbrook. Anyway, I'm supposed to be taking Cadno for a walk.'

'We'll join you then.'

Bryn called Cadno, and turned right at the main street to follow the road to Fox Lair Farm and the fields. He was aware that Carys was staring at him, her large eyes betraying no emotion. Maybe she had been talking to Selwyn, and saying he was dangerous was all an act. Maybe Selwyn was part of everything after all. Maybe there was no one to be trusted in Morredin. So many questions he wanted answered.

'Weird, wasn't it, the way the rain suddenly turned to hail?' said Bryn, watching Cadno race ahead as they turned into the path leading to the stream.

'A bit,' said Carys.

'A bit? I'd say it was bloody crazy, especially the size of the hail. Did you see what it did to those cars?' He looked at Carys. 'Anyway, Granddad told me it was written in that Revelation stuff in the bible. You know, the bit Miss Hughes got so excited about when she read it in church.'

'I'd forgotten that, Bryn. Still that just old words which

nobody takes any notice of.' She smiled briefly. 'No one really believes in that stuff about horses in the sky, and flaming mountains. Mind you, Miss 'raven-haired beauty' Hughes did get carried away didn't she?'

'Just supposing…'

'Supposing what?'

'Not important,' said Bryn, suddenly afraid to give more information. 'Look at Cadno, he's startled a rabbit.'

He watched his dog bark madly and hurtle across the stream, trying to catch the grey form that suddenly did a sharp turn to the right and disappear into a thick clump of gorse. Cadno dug his legs into the ground, but was unable to stop himself plunging into the tangle of growth with its sharp spines. He emerged, yelping with pain and slunk back to Bryn.

'Rabbits aren't as daft as you think,' Bryn said, kneeling down and picking some spines and yellow flowers from his dog's coat. He looked up at Carys. 'Bit surprising there's no foxes round here anymore, don't you think?'

'What makes you say that?'

'Well, the whole place is full of rabbits. Bet there's foxes a few miles from here.'

Carys shrugged her shoulders. 'Maybe they all died.' She stopped and turned round. 'We're going home now. See you tomorrow.'

Bryn watched them walk away. Gwyn's like a pet lamb, he thought. Doesn't say a word, and does everything she says. Bet he didn't want to go home. I think he'd like to talk to me, but is scared of Carys.

He waited until they had disappeared, then looked towards the wood that hid Selwyn's cottage from view. The old man wanted to meet him in about… he glanced at his watch. How times flies, he thought. Only another twenty minutes or so. Better get moving. Wonder what he wants to show me? Sounded important, and I bet it's to do with what's been happening round here.

'Come on Cadno, let's carry on walking.' Bryn looked at his dog, sitting with a front paw held forlornly in front of him. 'Got a thorn in your foot?' He knelt down and carefully pulled the offending item from between the pads. 'That'll teach you to chase rabbits.'

Bryn came to the stepping stones and sat down on the grass. He stared at the gurgling water glistening in the sunshine. It was amazing to think that only a few hours ago, the heavens had rained huge hailstones down. Turning his head, he stared at the brooding peaks of the Court of Foxes. The key to the weird events in Morredin lay somewhere in those hills. He was sure of it, just as he was sure his dreams were also, somehow, connected.

'Deep in thought again, Bryn. Just like that first time we met.'

'That's right, Selwyn,' said Bryn. He picked up a stone and flung it into the water, then watched the ripples extend from the splash as it sank. Turning round, he stared up at the solemn face of the old man.

'So much has happened here to me, and it's getting more frightening.'

'Come with me and maybe what I have to show you will elucidate the situation.'

Bryn frowned at the words, which did not make much sense. He wished Selwyn would not speak in such a weird manner. Calling Cadno as he stood up, Bryn brushed off the loose grass, and followed Selwyn who strode across the stones towards the distant wood.

Running to keep up with the large strides of his companion, Bryn felt that there would be no further conversation until the dwelling was reached. He smiled at Cadno, who darted into the thick bushes, and checked behind the trees, barking excitedly all the time.

Lucky dog, thought Bryn, no worries. All he has to do is have fun with regular meals. Even took to his name the first time I called him. But why did I call him 'Cadno'? Didn't even know what it meant until Granddad told me. Foxes, foxes, foxes. I'm beginning to hate the animal.

'Here we are,' said Selwyn, opening the gate to let Bryn and Cadno pass. Bryn waited until the cottage door was opened, then told Cadno to lie down outside.

'No need for him to stay outside, Bryn.' Selwyn stooped and stroked Cadno's head. 'Come and join us, furry friend.'

Bryn grinned as he read more biblical texts painted on the cottage walls, then followed Selwyn inside.

'Sit down, Bryn, and I'll make us some tea,' said Selwyn, then disappeared into his tiny kitchen.

Bryn slumped into the armchair and the warmth of the fire made his eyes droop until his head fell back and he was gently snoring in his sleep. He was wakened by a gentle shake of his shoulder, and turned his head to look up at the smiling face of the old man.

'Too many late nights?' said Selwyn, handing over a mug of steaming tea.

'Too many thoughts about this place, and this Emrys Morgan guy.'

Bryn then told Selwyn about his visit to the vicar and looking at the church records of the wedding of Emrys Morgan. He also mentioned the vicar had told him there was a son from the marriage.

Selwyn sat down and drank noisily, saying nothing. At last he placed his mug down by his side on the floor, and reached inside his parka.

Bryn watched him extract a photograph, stare at it, then at him. Selwyn repeatedly looked from photograph to Bryn, then shook his head.

'What is it?' said Bryn.

'This, my young friend, is a photograph that cannot exist.'

'Don't understand.'

'This is a picture taken of someone at a time when photography had not been invented,' said Selwyn. He tapped the photograph. 'But it does exist, as I have a copy in my hands.'

'Who is it?' said Bryn.

'You tell me,' said Selwyn, and passed the photograph over.

Bryn stared at the photo with mounting panic. He eyed the seated figure dressed in a black suit, with a striped cravat neatly tied round the high winged collar of his shirt. The carefully combed hair was parted in the centre. But it was the features that Bryn found disturbing.

He was hypnotised by the lean face, with tight lips, a long angular nose and dark brooding eyes. The eyebrows were like thick hedges as they met in the middle in an unbroken line. Bryn felt his heart lurch as he looked at the one feature he had forgotten when thinking about his father's appearance.

'You seem to recognise someone,' said Selwyn.

'That could be a photo of dad,' whispered Bryn. He turned his head to look at the old man. 'But it can't be, can it?'

'No, Bryn it can't be, for two reasons. First, that photo is impossible, because the subject is a young man, say, in his twenties.'

'Who is it?'

'I'm coming to that. That person died in 1840, aged fifty three, and the earliest known photograph was done in France and England around 1839. The Englishman was a man called Fox Talbot. Yet this picture exists, and this copy, which I have had for years, is in the National Archives of Wales.' Selwyn stood up and walked across to Bryn. Gently, he cupped the boy's chin so that their eyes met.

'I don't know what to believe, because unless this person came back from the dead, as a young man, this photograph cannot exist. And that is the second reason.'

'So who is this man, who looks so much like my dad?'

'Emrys Morgan.'

CHAPTER EIGHTEEN

Bryn slumped in the armchair, and his hands trembled as they clutched the photograph that could not exist. His eyes were moist, his heart thumping with the increasing panic.

How could this man, from so long ago, be the spitting image of his dad? How could dad look so like someone who was a wizard and a very evil man?

'But dad isn't even Welsh,' said Bryn, handing back the photograph. 'It must just be a …'

'Coincidence?' said Selwyn. 'Maybe, and maybe there is another explanation.'

'Don't understand.' Bryn was relaxing, his heartbeat returning to normal, and the panic attack subsiding.

'You may recall that you have just told me Emrys Morgan had a son by his wife.'

'So?'

'Just talking, Bryn, just talking. But it is incumbent on me to delve into what became of that poor woman. It is also important that I investigate your family history.'

'There isn't any,' said Bryn. 'Mum was born here, Granddad

also, and not much happened to anyone.'

'Not your mother, Bryn, but your father.'

'Dad?'

'Your dreams, the things you have seen in your nightmares, the strange weather that suddenly appears. All this happening since you came here. Morredin has been like a sleeping monster for years.' Selwyn's voice trembled with emotion. 'It is my comprehension that you are the link between this world and the world of the Great Dragon. How, I do not know at the moment, but I need to find out more of the history of your father.'

'Mum doesn't like talking about him, and Granddad won't.'

'Maybe, Bryn, but it is imperative I find out about his parents to begin my research.'

'Don't understand, but…' Bryn frowned in concentration. 'I know he was born in Derby, and Mum married him there. His parents lived there, and I think, can't be sure though, they were born there.'

'Let me get something to write with, then I can take it all down, and begin my investigation. You know your father's age and birthday?'

'Yes, but what's it got to do with anything?'

'I have my reasons, but will not impart them to you for the present. In the meantime,' said Selwyn, going to his desk and taking out a pencil and paper, 'Let us get some facts down.' Selwyn placed a hand across his mouth then pointed a finger at his guest. 'What we have discussed today must be our secret, and on no account tell anyone about this photograph.'

'Not even Mum?'

'No one.'

Selwyn listened and began to write as Bryn gave him information. Gentle probing by the old man triggered more information as he recalled more detail

Bryn finally left his seat and slowly walked to the door of the cottage. Cadno, glad to be on the move, barked his pleasure and ran out.

'May the protection of the Supreme Goodness be with you on your travels,' said Selwyn, placing his hands on Bryn's head, and looking skywards.

Bryn felt a sense of peace flowing through his body, like the warming rays of the sun. He was smiling again as he reached the gate, then stopped as a question sprang to mind.

'Selwyn, do you really think Emrys was, somehow, able to come back from the dead in order to have his photograph taken?'

'Yes, Bryn, I do. Cadno Du was no ordinary mortal, as I have told you.'

Bryn waved goodbye, then turned and slowly walked away from the cottage, down the path and into the wood. Cadno rushed round looking for rabbits, but his master was deep in thought.

I've seen a photo that couldn't have been taken. It's of a man who couldn't have been alive at the time. Now Selwyn tells me he came back from being dead to have it taken. Surely he can't still be around?

Bryn looked round, half expecting to see the black haired man in the ruffled collar spring out from behind a tree. He began to run with the sudden urge to move out of the wood as quickly as possible.

Reaching the stepping stones, he saw a familiar figure running along the path on the other side of the stream.

Idris turned his head and stopped when he saw Cadno splash across, followed by his master who jumped across the stones.

'Where have you been?' said Idris, wiping the sweat from his head. He was in his tracksuit and trainers, and took a swig from a small bottle of water he was holding.

'Been to see Selwyn.'

'What about?'

'Can't say. He told me not to.' Bryn watched Idris pick up a stone and skim it across the water. Cadno, thinking it a new game, rushed into the water, barking happily.

'He's a strange man, see, and you don't want to believe everything he says.' Idris turned his head to stare at Bryn with a dullness that gave no indication what he was thinking.

'But you like him, don't you?'

'He's all right. Not many like him in the village.'

'Maybe he knows too much,' said Bryn, staring at Idris, trying to see through his dark eyes, and find out what he was really thinking.

'About what?'

'The cave, for instance,' said Bryn. 'The cave that Carys and her friends go to, and…'

'Have you been there?' demanded Idris, swivelling round. His voice was hard, accusing and suspicious.

'Yes, and I think it was all a bit silly, speaking some rubbishy words and lighting candles.' Bryn was not going to give away any of his suspicions to Idris, not at the moment anyway. He needed to know more about him.

Stroking Cadno, who had come to his side, and began to vigorously shake the water from his coat, Bryn walked to the water's edge, and sat down.

'Have you been inside that cave, Idris?'

'Yes.'

'Are you in their gang?'

'No, and I wouldn't want to be.' Idris began to skim stones again, and his brow was furrowed in thought.

'What do you think they are saying?' Bryn casually glanced at his companion, and could see he was in turmoil. He knows more than he's prepared to say, thought Bryn. Bet he's been told a lot by Selwyn.

'Never heard them. Only went in the cave when no one was there.' He looked down at Bryn. 'Did you go with them?'

'Just once. Not sure why I was invited, but it was a bit scary.'

'In what way?'

'Well,' said Bryn, 'I thought that…' his voice trailed away as the memory of the ghostly hand on his shoulder came back. He shivered for a moment, then forced a smile. 'What I mean is, some of the words were weird, such as 'Adentium,' 'Mes… something or other.'

'Mesantium,' said Idris.

'How do you know?'

'That's only for me to know, see,' said Idris. 'Must go, supposed to be training.'

Before Bryn could respond, Idris had turned on his heel and sprinted away down the path.

'Well, Cadno, it all gets crazier and crazier.' Bryn stood up and watched Idris vanish round a bend. 'Come on, better get home before I'm in trouble again.'

A white rabbit appeared from behind a bush, and sat down. It began to wash its face, ignoring Cadno who sat down on his haunches, surprised to see the creature.

'Cadno, come here, boy,' ordered Bryn, as he began to trot down the path towards the village.

His dog had other ideas, and barked at the rabbit, which stopped washing, sniffed the air, and looked at Cadno. They stared at each other, then Cadno barked, which resulted in the rabbit leaping away in the opposite direction to Bryn.

'Cadno!' yelled Bryn, and turned to see his dog streaking down the path after the rabbit. 'Come back at once!'

His dog was in his element, chasing a rabbit. As the furry animal bounded down the path, Cadno hurtled in pursuit, barking his pleasure.

'Hell,' said Bryn, and ran after his disobedient hound. Down the path, the three raced, past the wood on the other side of the stream. The rabbit suddenly veered to its right and stopped by the path leading up the Court of Foxes.

As he ran, Bryn was panicking. It was as though the rabbit knew where it wanted to go. Why should a rabbit try and entice them to follow? And another thing. How weird to see a white rabbit out in the open. Wild rabbits were a dull grey. So what was this rabbit doing, and why decide to reveal itself to them?

As these worrying thoughts flooded through Bryn's mind, the rabbit turned and bounded up the path. Cadno followed, impervious to his master's shouts.

Bryn glanced at the sky as the wind strength increased. Clouds were thickening. The sun disappeared behind one large cloud, which increased in size. He looked up, stumbled, and cried out in fear.

The white cloud was gradually changing shape until it took the form of a prancing horse. As he watched, the cloud darkened and the white horse became an even larger black horse. His nightmares were returning.

Wisps of cottony fog were beginning to form. They rolled down the hillside, like writhing arms of a monster seeking its prey. The rabbit had stopped and reared up, checking to ensure it was still being followed.

Bryn called to his dog again. This was no ordinary rabbit. They were being encouraged to follow, but for what reason?

As he followed the two animals up the hillside, then along the path to the Wizard Rock, Bryn was consumed with fear. He didn't want to continue, but could not leave his dog. The rabbit, or whatever creature had taken that form, knew he would follow Cadno. It washed its face again, waiting until the dog was near, then bounded away.

Thunder rolled round the hills, and the sun had finally disappeared, the black clouds thickened and blotting out its warmth. Bryn shivered as the wind increased.

How could the weather change so quickly from a warm, sunny afternoon to a banshee wind, increasing darkness, and a mind-numbing cold? This was not natural. He had been enticed onto those hills for a purpose. What purpose?

Bryn looked at the Wizard Rock, frightened at events he could not control. That stone knew so many secrets. It had witnessed evil. The wisps of fog had become thick strands that curled round him and the stone. He was embraced in an ever- thickening band of damp swirling greyness that blanked out the view. Yet the area round the stone on which he stood was clear. This was a fog that defied logic.

'Cadno!' screamed Bryn, terrified to move from his strange prison. The wind changed to a choir of voices from hell. Bryn had heard that sound before, and knew the words, "Adentium'", "Mesantium".

'Cadno, answer me, please,' cried Bryn, and sank to his knees, sobbing in desperation.

An answering bark made him look up, and the wall of swirling fog parted to reveal a way up the hill. As his gaze lifted, Bryn could see Cadno, a long way up the sheer hillside. Above him sat the white rabbit, which changed to a fox as Bryn stared in horror. Even worse was the colour. He was looking at a black fox.

Bryn rubbed his eyes and gazed again at the creature. It was once again a white rabbit, and darted nimbly up the hillside, followed by Cadno.

Vainly calling his dog, Bryn scrambled up the rocky face, grabbing clumps of gorse to haul himself upwards. His hands were soon bleeding, and sweat poured out of him with the exertion. The climb was becoming very steep, and he slipped back several times, arms outstretched, hands grasping grass, rocky outcrops, anything to halt the slide.

He glanced behind and the fog had closed across the way back. There was only one way to go now: upwards, and follow the rabbit.

The animal had reached a small tree, growing tenuously out of an outcrop. Its twisted branches were denuded of leaves, and the gnarled bark a deep brown. Bryn guessed it would have been invisible from below. He had no idea where they were, or how long he had been climbing. His arms and legs ached, and his jeans were torn.

Cadno, tongue lolling in his mouth, crawled up to the rabbit, which stared down disdainfully, nose twitching.

A peal of thunder rattled round the hills, as the rabbit hopped up to the tree, then disappeared. Cadno followed, and Bryn then heard his dog bark. He forced his aching limbs to move, urged on by the notion that Cadno's barking appeared to come from somewhere inside the hill.

Grasping the trunk of the tree with outstretched bleeding hands, Bryn hauled himself to his feet, and stood for a moment, chest heaving as he gasped for breath.

Carefully, he stepped round the tree, knowing that one false move could send him hurtling down the hill. Stones rattled loose under his feet as he inched his way round.

A waft of cold air greeted him as he finally eased round the outcrop. His heart raced as he saw a cleft in the rock face, and another bark from Cadno made him move.

His dog had entered into the hill through that cleft. Bryn followed, with increasing trepidation. There was danger within, but he had no option. Of one thing Bryn was sure. Through that gash in the hillside lay a route to a cave.

The entrance was overgrown with scrub, which clung to sheets of blue grey slabs of rock, laid on each other like slate tiles on cottage roofs. Small stalactites festooned the surface, like icy lace.

'Cadno, here, boy,' called Bryn, more in hope than expectation. He was answered by a bark. Cadno appeared to have stayed in one spot.

Stomach rumbling, Bryn took a deep breath then stepped through the entrance. The atmosphere was oppressive and terrifying. He slowly moved further into the cave, taking a familiar downward path. Bryn had entered his nightmare.

As he turned a corner, he found his eyes becoming used to the gloom. A ghostly blue light emanated from the walls, which glistened from the damp. It was increasingly cold, and he shivered.

Cadno was sitting on the ground, wagging his tail feebly when he saw his master. The rabbit had vanished, its work done. Bryn was on a journey he had dreamed about since moving to Morredin.

'Come on, Cadno. I must go on now.' Bryn did not know exactly where he was going, as his dreams only took him so far on the journey. He was sure of one thing: there was something important, something mind-boggling, waiting for him.

When he touched the cave walls, he recoiled from the cold. He could see his breath escaping, like steam from a kettle, as it rose from his open mouth. Cadno walked by his side as he crunched his way over stones and pieces of fallen rock.

On and on he slowly walked, the path leading ever downwards, until it turned abruptly to the right, and a wider chamber. Warm air filled the interior.

His knees buckled as he entered, and he cried out in terror. The chamber was oval in shape, with a slab of rock in the centre. A blue light encased the rock, which pulsated with an inner energy.

But it wasn't that sight which made Cadno howl, and Bryn sink to his knees and scream again and again, 'No! No!'

In the middle of the rock lay a dusty, old, brown leather-bound book. Secured by several gold padlocks, a set of keys lay beside it.

Bryn did not have to count to know the number of padlocks was seven.

CHAPTER NINETEEN

Bryn stared at the book, his skin clammy with fear. He had only half believed Selwyn when talking about a book of seven keys, which contained malevolent power. Now it lay before him on a slab of stone, much like the altar on the hill.

Cadno crawled beside him, whimpering and shivering. His canine senses told him that there was danger in this chamber.

'Don't believe what I'm seeing,' said Bryn, and cuddled his dog. He tried to look away from the book, but was increasingly drawn back to stare at the cracked leather binding.

Without thinking, he stood up and walked to the stone and stared down at the book. Slowly he extended an arm and let his hand touch the volume. A powerful burst of energy shot up from the book through his arm, like an electric current.

Bryn tried to take his hand away as he screamed out. It appeared to be glued to the cover, and unable to control events, he placed his other hand on the book.

He writhed from the force emanating from the leather. The book was glowing and pulsating with energy. A familiar voice intruded into his mind.

'Now you know your destiny. You are the chosen one.'

As he screamed out at the pain, Bryn felt his body burning with the heat of the force that had transferred from the book. He looked at his exposed arms and hands. They were bright red, and the skin rippled with a life of its own.

There was a moment's relief, then he felt a surge of power and energy rush from himself, down his arms, and into the book. He was being drained by an unstoppable torrent.

Sweat, mingled with tears, oozed down Bryn's face, and he could hear Selwyn in the background urging him to fight. He had a choice, good or evil.

'Won't, won't,' cried Bryn, and as Selwyn's voice grew stronger in his mind, he focussed on his hands.

I can let go of this book if I want to, he thought. It's only an old dusty book. How can it force me to hold it if I don't want to? I won't listen to that other voice. Selwyn is my friend. He will protect me. Now I will let go and leave this place.

Bryn focussed on his arms, as his strength diminished. Lifting his hands from the leather, calmness coursed through him like a smoothly flowing river. He collapsed on the ground, drained of energy, and cried with relief at breaking the spell that had bound him to the book.

Exhaustion overcame him, and he drifted into a fitful slumber. He had no idea how long he had been asleep, but woke up, stiff and thirsty.

'Let's go, Cadno,' said Bryn, and grimaced, forcing stiff and aching limbs to move. He retraced his steps to the entrance, then stopped.

Thunder crackled overhead, and a thick fog swirled across the cleft in the hill face. A gale screamed outside, yet the fog stayed: a thick impenetrable blanket.

He was trapped. To try and find his way down the hill would be dangerous. Until the fog cleared he was forced to stay where he was.

Bryn shivered with the cold permeating through the gloom. He turned and slowly walked back down the passage. Cadno trotted beside him, sensing his master was troubled.

As they walked into the chamber and the warmth, Bryn realised another power had changed the weather to force him to stay in the cave. The warmth of the chamber ensured he would return to the book of seven locks.

'Mum will be going crazy,' said Bryn, glancing at his watch. 'I should have been home ages ago. What am I going to do, Cadno?'

He sat down on the floor, with his back to the wall. Cadno lay down, placed his head on Bryn's leg and whined.

'Getting hungry?' said Bryn, and felt in his jean's pockets. He smiled as his fingers felt some wrapped toffees. Cadno lifted his head and wagged his tail.

'Bad for your teeth, but better than nothing,' said Bryn, and unwrapped two, giving one to his dog.

As he slowly chewed, Bryn looked round. The chamber was small, and whereas the rocky walls were the same blue grey colour of the passage, the stone in the centre was dark green and purple. He wondered if that stone had been brought into the cave. But how could they drag it up the hillside, he thought?

'Magic forces, Cadno,' said Bryn, and forced a laugh. He didn't really think it funny, but was trying to give himself courage to face a long stay in the cave.

His eyes were drawn back to the book, and without thinking, stood up and walked to the stone. The texture of the leather had changed. It was no longer cracked and wrinkled, but smooth and polished. Gingerly, he extended an arm and touched the leather binding. There was no electric shock, no surge of power hurtling through him. But that malevolent voice was in his mind again, this time soft and coaxing.

'I mean you no harm, Bryn. Pick up the book. Open it if you like, and read the wisdom, the power over the Universe contained within.'

Bryn picked up the glistening bunch of keys, and felt the cold smooth lustre of the gold. He then let the fingers of one hand slide over each lock. It would be so easy to open this book and see what was inside. What would be the harm? It was not as if he really believed in anything to do with religion. Even Selwyn had said he did not believe in a God who looked like an old man with a long beard.

'But he does believe in something, Cadno,' said Bryn, looking down at his dog who had come to his side. 'He thinks something terrible is about to happen here, and it's got something to do with that book, and me.'

Bryn put the keys back on the stone, and walked out of the chamber. He was thirsty and walked along the passage. Seeing a rivulet running down the wall, he cupped a hand to collect some of the water, and drank it. Water had never tasted so good, and Cadno eagerly drank from the pool on the floor.

'Let's go back to the warm cave. Reckon we're here for the night.' Bryn looked at the fog still obscuring the entrance. 'Can't see that going quickly. Mum will be sick with worry, and Granddad will be losing his cool.'

As he settled down in the chamber, with Cadno cuddled up against him, Bryn suddenly realised that he had been able to walk away from the book. He had a choice. No power made him stay or open the padlocks. Yet Selwyn had told him this was a book written by an evil power. He had also been told that everyone had a choice between good and evil. Who or what was the 'Supreme Goodness'?

Bryn fought tiredness for some time, then as fatigue overcame his resistance he fell asleep, his arms wrapped round his dog for mutual warmth and comfort. His last thought, before his mind switched off, was a vision of two faces side by side, Emrys and his father.

He stared up at the rocky ceiling, and lay still, trying to focus his thoughts. Slowly he brought an arm across so that he could see his watch.

'It's after seven, Cadno,' said Bryn, and shivered. The heat had gone from the chamber, and the glow from the walls was dim. Whatever power had been present to encourage him to enter had gone. It was as though a mission has been accomplished.

Bryn glanced at the book, and scrambled to his feet. He had the uncomfortable feeling that events had begun which he could not change.

As his eyes became accustomed to the gloom, he walked out of the chamber and along the passage, feeling his way along the cold and damp walls.

The fog had gone, and a faint mist greeted him as he reached the entrance. He peered over the edge and gasped. The hillside dropped steeply away, and the path was just a faint, snaking thread far below.

Did I really climb up so high yesterday, he thought? It's not going to be easy getting down again.

He felt in a pocket and found his two last toffees, giving one to Cadno. Chewing thoughtfully, he glanced back down the passage. There was so much to think about, apart from what he was going to say to his mother.

All my nightmares were about this cave, and the book of seven locks. It's almost a relief to have found it, but what do I do now? Can't tell Mum or Granddad. Not yet anyway. Need time to think. What would happen if I opened it? Would horrible creatures fly out? Or would I be able to summon terrible beasts with amazing powers? Sounds too frightening. Maybe I'd better keep it to myself.

He watched Cadno carefully walk down the slope and followed, grasping the tree branches before easing himself away from the cleft.

Bryn found it easier to sit down and use his legs to control a slide over the rocks and loose stones. A ripping sound told him that the seat of his jeans had given way. He glanced at the rips in the legs and wondered how he would explain it to his mother.

'That's nothing compared to trying to explain where I was last night,' he said to Cadno, who was sitting on his haunches, waiting for his master to join him.

'I don't know what I'm going to say. Must see Selwyn and tell him. He'll know what to do.'

He slipped and slid down the hillside. A chatter overhead made him look up. A slowly moving helicopter was circling the area. Bryn waved, then heard shouts nearby as the machine moved away. As he listened, he could hear his name being called over and over.

'I'm here,' he yelled, and waved his arms. The movement made his feet lose their grip, and he tumbled, over and over, down the hill, until he lay in a crumpled unconscious heap on the path.

Cadno whined, and licked his face, until Bryn came round and sat up. His head was spinning, as he wiped dirt and grass from his hair, and looked at the tears in his shirt.

'I'm in dead trouble now,' he said to his dog.

'I wouldn't be at all surprised,' said Bob Holbrook, walking towards him with another villager.

CHAPTER TWENTY

Bryn ladled the cornflakes from his bowl, and slowly ate. Lying in bed with a tray balanced on his legs was not easy. Spooning the cereal without spilling any on the bedclothes was harder. He thought back to when he was found by one of the search parties.

Events, since being found, had hurtled along. Bob Holbrook had called others on his mobile phone, then tried to make him comfortable.

An ambulance had motored as far as possible along the path, then the crew had walked the rest of the way, carrying a stretcher.

Bryn grimaced as he was carefully lifted from the ground. He ached everywhere from the tumbling descent down the hillside. Cadno trotted behind the men as his master was carefully carried to the ambulance.

Siren blaring, the vehicle proceeded down the path, and into the village. Bryn drifted in and out of consciousness as he was taken to the hospital in town. He had little recollection of events after that, as he was examined, x-rayed and checked through the day. Time passed slowly as various doctors came, looked into his eyes, checked his reflexes and wrote notes.

'When can I go home?' he asked a nurse who came to take his temperature. She glared when he took the thermometer out of his mouth.

'When the doctors say you can, Bryn. After all, you don't seem to remember much of what happened, do you?'

'It's a bit hazy, that's all,' said Bryn, keeping his thoughts to himself. He remembered every detail of the cave and the magic book inside.

I musn't tell anyone, he thought. There's only one person I want to speak to as soon as I get home. Selwyn must know quickly. He waited until the nurse glanced at the thermometer, and nodded her satisfaction.

'You'll live, young man.'

'I did take a helluva tumble,' said Bryn. 'Not surprising I can't remember much.'

The nurse smiled, plumped up his pillows and walked across the ward to the bed opposite.

As he finished his cereal, Bryn looked round his bedroom. It was great to be home, even though he still ached. The tests had shown there were no broken bones or torn muscles, and his scan suggested he had no head injuries. The consultant had told him he was being kept in for the night for observation, but should be home the next morning.

Visits from his tearful mother and grandfather, coupled with concerned comments from them, both had helped him recover. No questions about the previous night had aided recovery. Now he was home, wallowing in the attention of his family.

'How are you feeling now,' said his mother, pushing open the door, and sitting on his bed. 'Enjoy your breakfast?'

'Great, thanks, Mum,' said Bryn. 'Don't know why they kept me in hospital all day. Anyone would have had bruises after falling down that hill. It was a long way down.'

'It wasn't just the fall, Bryn.'

'What then?'

'It's what you said on your way in the ambulance, son,' said Gareth walking in, followed by Cadno.

'What did I say?'

'You said you became lost when a thick fog came down suddenly.'

'So?'

'Because there wasn't a fog yesterday in the hills. Thunder, maybe, and the sky blackened, but definitely no fog.'

Bryn turned his face to the wall so that they could not see his red face, and mumbled, 'Well it was foggy where I was, and I couldn't see a thing.'

'I'm not going to argue with you, young man, but the whole village was out in the hills last night looking for you.'

'Sorry about that,' said Bryn, 'But I didn't hear anyone.'

'Didn't you see the torches, there were dozens?' said his mother.

'Told you, it was foggy, Mum.' Bryn turned to look at his mother. 'Why doesn't anyone believe me?'

'It's just that, as Granddad said, there was no fog here, which poses the question, where were you?'

'Another planet?' Bryn tried to grin, but his bruised face made him say, 'Ouch,' instead.

'Probably,' said his mother. She smiled, kissed him on the top of his head, and took his tray from him. 'I'll leave you now, to have more rest.'

'Lot to think about,' said Bryn, to Cadno, lying by his bed, as the door was closed. He leaned over and pulled his notebook from under the mattress.

I must get it all down while it's still fresh in my mind. No one's going to believe anything, 'cept Selwyn, and maybe Idris. What about Carys and her friends? Would they believe I've found the secret book? Then there's 'Raven-haired beauty,' Miss Hughes.

He chewed on the end of his pen for a moment, and quickly covered the pages with everything that happened after he left Idris, and the appearance of the rabbit.

Tiredness swept over him in waves, and he fought to keep his eyes open as he finished writing. He began reading from the beginning, and shook his head to try and keep awake. Sleep would not be denied, and Bryn let his notebook slip from his hands, and settled back on his pillows.

He struggled with a vivid dream and thrashed around in bed. Once again he was on the windswept Court of Foxes, in the hollow, and standing by the altar stone. Sitting in a circle round him were dozens of foxes and their leader, a huge black animal, walked towards him. It reared up on its hind legs and changed into a young Emrys Morgan.

He smiled at Bryn, picked up a thick, leather-bound book from the stone, and offered it to Bryn, only to snatch it back again. Shaking his head, Emrys opened the book and began to read.

'No! No!' cried Bryn. 'That book is mine. You can't read it.' He rushed forwards, and grappled with Emrys, grabbing the book with both hands. A familiar voice intruded on his dream, and brought him back to reality.

'Bryn, what's the matter with you?' said his mother, as he snatched his notebook from her. 'I was only tidying up.'

Bryn stared at her, wild-eyed and heart pounding. He clutched the notebook tightly to his chest, trying to get some semblance of order in his mind.

'Sorry, Mum, having a bad dream again.' He tried to sound casual. 'Didn't read any, did you?'

'No. Should I have done?'

'It's my secret diary, and I don't share my secrets with anyone.'

'Not even Cadno?' smiled his mother.

'That's different, 'cos I know he won't tell anyone.'

'I'll leave you now to get some rest, as a lot of people want to see you.'

'Who?' said Bryn, sitting up.

'Well, let's see. There are your friends at school, Carys, Gwyn. Even Idris came round asking after you, which surprised me. I thought you two didn't get on. Then there was Mr Price, your teacher, and Selwyn…'

'Selwyn came round? What did he say?'

'Said he wanted to come back when you felt better. Something important to tell you. Not sure how we'll get Granddad to let him in.' His mother walked to the door, then turned round, and stared at her son.

'What?' said Bryn.

'Bryn, I did see the first sentence in your book. Could hardly miss it as you'd written it in block capitals. What does "the book really exists. I've seen it", mean?'

'Rather not say, Mum.'

'Have it your way, Bryn,' said his mother, and left the room.

'Parents!' cried Bryn to Cadno, who thrust his head into his master's hand. 'They are a pain. Want to know everything that doesn't concern them. Pity mum saw that sentence, but did she read more than she's telling?'

He eased himself out of bed, and for a moment the room was spinning. Clutching the bed for support, Bryn waited until his head cleared then walked to the window.

Looking out at the distant hills, the peaks of Court of Foxes stood out, sharp and menacing. So many mysteries out there, and now he had found the book of seven locks.

Must get dressed, thought Bryn. So much to do, and so much to tell Selwyn when he comes.

Slowly and painfully, he took off his pyjamas and put on his clothes, then left his bedroom. As he descended the stairs, he could hear voices, and recognised the laughter of Hugh Price.

'There you are,' said Hugh, and walked towards Bryn, saying, 'Oh dear, oh dear.' He bent down and squinted at Bryn's bruised face, then looked up towards Gareth.

'Out all night in the hills, you say?'

'That's right,' said Gareth. 'Hadn't a clue where he was, and said he couldn't get down because of the fog. Mind you, I think he took such a tumble down the hillside, his memory's playing tricks.'

'Were you very high up, Bryn?' said Hugh.

'Can't remember.'

'But you must have sheltered somewhere for the night.'

'Can't remember.'

Bryn watched his teacher stroke his chin, as he stared down. As though coming to a decision, Hugh Price smiled, and patted Bryn on the head, then turned on his heel.

'I'll go now, Mr Powell. Don't send him back to school until he's ready.'

'Knowing Bryn, I doubt if that'll be quick,' grinned Gareth as he opened the door for him to leave the cottage.

'Seems a nice teacher you've got there,' said Gareth.

'Hm,' said Bryn.

'What does that mean?'

'Nothing,' said Bryn, and shivered as he recalled the look in the teacher's eyes when being questioned. He had never seen such coldness in anyone's eyes before. It was frightening the way Hugh Price had looked at him.

'Where's Mum?' he asked, trying to get the image out of his mind.

'Nipped out to the corner shop for a few things.' Gareth looked at his grandson, the concern showing in his eyes.

'How are you really feeling, Bryn? Memory still playing tricks?'

'Ache a bit, but not too bad.' Bryn walked to the front door, and opened it. He closed his eyes and let the crisp air waft round his face. The smells of the fields, flowers, and the warmth of the setting sun were in sharp contrast to the cold dankness of the cave. He wondered if he could find the entrance again.

'Deep in thought?' said a familiar voice, and Bryn opened his eyes to see the amused expression in Selwyn's face.

'Selwyn!' cried Bryn, and rushed forwards to be enveloped in the old man's arms.

'Are you able to come for a short walk?' Selwyn looked up to see Gareth standing in the doorway, arms folded, his face showing hostility.

'Can Selwyn come in, Granddad?'

'He's not welcome in my house.'

'In that case, tell Mum I won't be long.'

'You come back in at once, Bryn. That's an order,' Gareth began to stride down the path.

'Let's go,' said Bryn, and walked along the path, turning right into the road. Selwyn strode by his side, saying nothing.

They walked in silence, crossed the main road, then ambled across the field to reach the flowing water. Cadno barked, and raced across to join them.

'You were in great danger last night, Bryn. I felt it,' said Selwyn. 'I tried to contact you by telepathy.'

'By what?'

Selwyn briefly smiled. 'In times of danger, people have been known to reach each other by using the hidden powers of the mind.'

'Maybe it worked, 'cos I thought I heard you when I was in the cave.'

'What cave?' said Selwyn, grasping Bryn's shoulder. 'What cave are you talking about?'

Bryn stopped walking and sank to his knees on the grassy bank. He gazed at the rushing water, and the dancing reflected light, like so many glistening diamonds.

Selwyn could see the fear in Bryn's face when he turned to look up at him, and sat down by his side.

'What is it, Bryn? Tell me all.' He chuckled for a moment. 'I seem to remember saying something like that when we first met.'

'I found it.'

'Found what.'

'The book of seven locks, Selwyn, and I'm scared. Very scared.'

Selwyn laid his staff on the ground, and steepled his hands under his chin. His blue eyes stared into space as he thought about the stunning news.

'Bryn, it is imperative that you remember every detail of your journey yesterday.' Selwyn's voice was trembling, as he continued to gaze at the opposite bank.

'It all began when Cadno chased the rabbit along this path, then up the hill,' began Bryn, closing his eyes to try and recall events.

'A rabbit began everything?'

'Yes, Selwyn. Looking back, I don't think that rabbit was an ordinary bunny. It seemed too clever, as though it knew what it wanted. I believe that rabbit was…'

'Not there by accident, but sent by Cadno Du, the Black Fox,' whispered Selwyn.

'Dunno about that. All I know is, it seemed to tease Cadno into chasing it. Up and up we climbed.'

Selwyn listened quietly, as the story unfolded. Only when he heard of the discovery of the magical book did he sit up straight and stare, unblinkingly, at Bryn.

'What was the state of the book when you found it?'

'All cracked, dirty, and covered in dust. That was until I touched it. Didn't want to, Selwyn, but something or somebody, made me. I could, sort of, hear that voice telling me to pick it up.'

'You-picked-it–up?'

'Couldn't help myself, and it was scary what happened. Felt like 'lectricity coming from the book up my arms, then it seemed all my strength left me. It went into the book.' Bryn wiped the tears flooding down his face with his arm. 'Don't remember anything after that. Think I must have fainted.'

'When you were awake later, did you notice anything changed?'

Bryn screwed up his face, and nodded. 'The book had changed. It now looked as if someone had put a new cover on. The leather was smooth, glossy, and smelt of polish.'

'As I feared, as I feared,' muttered Selwyn, rocking back and forwards. He turned to Bryn. 'You were the instrument to bring to life the evil contained in the pages of the book. That I know and have confirmed with my research of the history of your family.'

'What about my family?'

'I might not be a young man anymore, but have made myself learn about the marvels in technology today. Computers are a miracle, and the Internet a blessing. I began by going as far back as I could in the local records. I believe you know that Emrys Morgan had a son, and his mother fled the family home, taking him.'

'What's that got to do with me? Anyway, I'm from Derby, and so's Dad.'

'Patience, young man, because I had to have it in abundance during my research. When the wife of Emrys learned she was a widow, you can imagine the joy in her heart. She was free, at last, from that malevolent being, and could make a new life for herself and her child.

That was where I had to search and search, to find out what happened. She did re-marry, and had more children, six in fact. But, and this is important, Bryn, she had no more boys, so I continued with her son's life.'

'Was he like…?'

'Was he like his father, you were about to ask?' Selwyn shook his head. 'I learned he became a farmer, married, and also had two sons. He lived in Mid Wales, and there were never any stories about black magic, or any sort of magic. Gareth Lloyd was a pillar of society, a regular churchgoer, and very respected in his village. I realised there had to be a link with Emrys for his spirit to come back and continue Satan's mission. And I think you know what that link is.'

'The same birthday.' Bryn whispered. He felt the blood drain from his face, and rocked on his heels.

'Over the years, other sons were born, and one of your forebears did move to Derby to work in the new Rolls Royce factory. But even he, like your father, was not born on December the seventh. So, when your mother returned to Morredin, the circle was complete.'

Bryn threw a pebble into the stream, and thought what Selwyn had been saying. He watched the ever-widening circles from the splash in silence. I never wanted to come to this crazy village. Why me? I never asked to be related to a monster. I'm not going to help this ghost, but what if I am really like the Black Fox?

He tugged at Selwyn's sleeve. 'He is a ghost, isn't he? Even though I think I've seen him. I've certainly heard him, and his laugh is real scary.'

'A ghost? I think the Black Fox is more than just a ghost. I believe his spirit is more that just a wisp. He is powerful, and is close to crossing over from his present world to ours.'

Selwyn's voice shook with emotion. He threw his staff on the ground, and knelt in front of Bryn and held his face with his powerful hands.

'Bryn, time is short. Even now, he plans his final moves to bring chaos to our world. You have to return to that cave and bring me the book. I know what to do.'

'Don't want to go back. Not sure if I could find it again.'

'You will, and you must,' said Selwyn, his eyes burning with zeal. He groaned as he used the staff to force himself upright. 'Bring that accursed book to me at the weekend. Try and behave normally with everyone. There are those who are aware something momentous has happened, and they know it has something to do with you.'

Selwyn strode away, then stopped to give one last warning before striding across the stepping stones. His words sent shivers down Bryn's spine.

CHAPTER TWENTY-ONE

Bryn walked through the school gates and looked round at the faces of his fellow pupils. Some smiled, and waved a greeting, while a few ambled across and asked how he was feeling after his night adventures.

'Not too bad,' said Bryn to one boy in his class, and eased his rucksack off his back. He scanned the playground, looking for Carys and her friends.

'Didn't think you'd come back this week,' said the boy. 'I'd have made any excuse not to come to school.'

'Got bored,' said Bryn, seeing Carys near the school main door. She turned her head, and nodded, then said something to her friends and began to stroll across.

'Anyway, it's Saturday tomorrow.' Bryn saw Carys smile and wave.

'See you,' he said and walked across the playground.

'Do you still hurt?' said Carys as Bryn joined her. She stared at him with wide eyes, devoid of expression.

'Surprised you asked, considering you never came round to see me.'

'Don't like illness, see. Anyway, I bet you had lots of visitors.'

'Oh, yes, including Farty Price. Asked a lot of questions about what happened.'

'So how did you get lost in the hills?'

Bryn shrugged his shoulders. 'Haven't a clue. All I remember is Cadno chasing a rabbit, and me trying to call him back.'

'You must remember... have some idea where you were.'

'Carys, just listen,' said Bryn, anger rising in him. 'I have no idea. I'm fed up with everyone questioning me.'

Carys stared at him for a moment, and forced a smile. 'I bet you do really, just not saying.'

'Suit yourself,' said Bryn, and turning on his heel, trotted away, kicking the stones on the path in frustration. Girls! Not like us at all. Even got different minds. 'Stead of asking how I am, she has to ask questions. Anyway, she couldn't have been that worried, not coming to see me. Don't believe that crap about not liking illness. Does she think I enjoyed falling down the hill, and aching everywhere?

Bryn saw Gwyn push through a group of children and reach his side.

'Sorry I didn't come round,' he said, and stared at the ground.

'It's alright, Gwyn. No one seemed bothered, 'cept old Farty, and he only asked stupid questions.'

'It's not that I didn't want to, just that Carys said...' Gwyn stopped walking and glanced at Bryn. 'She's frightened of you.'

'What?' Bryn laughed. 'Carys frightened of me? I don't think anything can frighten her.'

The clanging of a handbell made all the children amble towards the main door. Anwen Hughes glared at the throng as she slowly moved her arm up and down, bringing the dull, mourneful sounds out of the bell.

As Bryn passed her, she allowed a ghost of a smile to cross her thin lips, and stopped ringing the bell.

'Bryn, welcome back. I really am surprised to see you, but delighted to see you restored to health. We were all so worried when you went missing that night.'

Bryn could only stare, open mouthed, at the teacher. Could this really be 'raven-haired beauty' Miss Hughes, who could see you, even when her eyes seemed to be looking elsewhere? Was this the same teacher who had no sense of humour, and regarded her pupils as pests?

'Much better now, Miss,' stammered Bryn. 'Still a few aches, but it was boring at home.'

'Ah,' smiled Miss Hughes. 'I thought, just for a moment, you were actually missing school.'

'No, Miss,' said Bryn, and hurried past to join the others in the main corridor as they made their way to the small hall and assembly, before classes commenced.

As they entered their classroom, Bryn clutched Gwyn's arm and spun him round.

'Why is Carys frightened of me?'

'Not sure, but…'

'Well?'

'She says something's been happening here ever since you came to live in Morredin.'

'Such as?'

'She says she felt something powerful in the cave that day you came. Told me afterwards she'd never felt that before. Said she looked at you, and thought you also felt something. And that was why you ran out. Did you?'

'Didn't feel anything, just thought it was all stupid,' said Bryn, trying to stop his rising panic. 'When did she start those crazy mumbo-jumbo meetings in that cave?'

'She didn't. Her dad knew about it from his dad.' Gwyn lowered his voice.

'Seems it's always been there, but only a few go. You have

to be invited.'

'So how come you were invited to join?'

'No idea. Carys invited me, just like she did you.'

'Hm,' mumbled Bryn, and ambled to his desk, then winced as his leg hit the chair. His bruises were still in evidence, a reminder of his accident.

'Right, children, settle down and we'll begin,' said Hugh Price, rapping his desk to gain attention. He waited until his class was sitting down, and voices became hushed.

'Good,' he beamed, and the familiar explosion erupted behind him, with accompanying chuckles from some of the children.

'I don't know what you find so funny,' said Hugh, tapping some exercise books on his desk. 'I can assure you I didn't find your anaemic efforts at the simple Geography task given either funny or satisfying.' He looked at Bryn. 'The only person here who did not test my patience was Bryn.'

'But I've been away, Sir.'

'Exactly,' sighed Hugh, and picked up the first book from the pile, and looked across at one boy, sitting on the back row. 'Gareth, do you have bad eyesight, or a problem co-ordinating your fingers? I give you the outline of the country, then ask you to colour in various parts. But you seem to have decided there was a landslip, and the green fields extend into the surrounding ocean.'

He extended an arm to Gwyn, who could not contain his laughter. 'I don't know why you are laughing.' The teacher shuffled through the books, then pulled one out and held it aloft.

'Ah, here we have Gwyn's effort, which I can only describe as a miserable, melancholy piece of memorabilia, to be instantly forgotten.'

Bryn listened to the teacher dismissing every piece of homework in similar fashion, which soon had the class quiet, even though the children had no idea what the long words meant. Something's put him in a foul mood. Maybe he ate something last night that's upset him. Maybe he had a row with his wife, 'cept he hasn't got one. Beginning to wish I'd stayed at home now, instead of listening to old Farty ranting on. Just hope this aching goes away in my legs. Got a hard climb tomorrow.

As his mind dwelled on his mission the following day, Bryn had a moment of panic. What if he couldn't find his way back to the cave where the secret book lay?

He tried to concentrate on the lesson, but his mind wandered back to the chase up the hill by Cadno. Gradually the droning voice of Hugh Price receded in Bryn's mind, and he found himself sketching on a page torn from his exercise book. As his pencil made a rough drawing of the Court of Foxes, he concentrated on the path his dog had taken.

'What are you drawing?' said Carys, intruding into his concentration. She leaned across to get a closer look.

'Nothing, really,' said Bryn, screwing up the paper and quickly opening his desk, threw the crumpled drawing inside.

The rest of the school day passed slowly for Bryn. As the time passed, his mind was concentrating on his task the following day. The sound of the bell ending the final class was a relief, and he hurried out of school and ran down the path.

As he turned into the road, he stopped and felt in his pockets for the sketch of the hills. The sketch was missing. He turned and sprinted back to the school gates.

'What's the matter?' said Carys, as he ran past. She was still inside the playground with a group of girls. 'Lose something?'

Bryn stopped, and stared at her smiling face.

'What did you say?'

'I asked if you've lost something.'

'Maybe.' said Bryn, and ran into the school, turned right, then headed for his classroom. Quickly opening his desk, Bryn looked for his sketch, and turfed books aside in his feverish search. The crumpled piece of paper was missing.

He stared at the open desk, trying to control his alarm. Did he take it out, and drop it somewhere? Think, Bryn, think, he said to himself, as he slowly lowered the desk top.

Walking out of the classroom, he passed Miss Hughes who tapped her watch and warned him the school was closing.

'Forgot something,' said Bryn, and began to run down the corridor.

'Walk!' commanded the teacher.

'Yes, Miss,' muttered Bryn, forcing himself to slow down until he exited the main door. He hurtled out of the school gates, turned right, then stopped as he saw a group ahead.

He wasn't surprised to see Carys, Gwyn and others in a huddle. What he did think unsual was to see them surrounding Mr Price, straddled across his bicycle.

'Ah, Bryn,' said the teacher, as he approached the group. 'I trust we shall see you again on Monday.'

'Yes, sir.'

'No wandering round the hills, I trust.' Hugh Price glanced at the distant range, bathed in the afternoon sunlight. 'Even though it looks enticing. Can be dangerous up there, as you well know. No wonder stories abound of spirits, evil forces and other horrors wandering round those slopes.'

'Just staying home and going to the match,' Bryn grimaced. 'As I can't play for them, might as well watch.'

'Good,' said the teacher, and waved as Bryn walked away.

Bryn walked along the path by the gurgling waters with his knapsack across his shoulders. Saturday morning had passed achingly slowly, despite the sun blazing in a blue sky. He had decided not to talk to his mother again about her reading his secret notebook.

As she had not brought up the subject of its contents, Bryn reasoned that maybe she had only read the first few sentences. They would not have given her much of an inkling of the drama unfolding in the pages.

After lunch, he had told her he was going for a walk, and when he laced on his boots, his mother had looked at him, frowning.

'Taking Cadno?'

'Not this time, mum. Meeting someone.'

'Who?'

'Idris,' said Bryn, surprised that he had named the older boy.

'Thought he wasn't friendly to you. Didn't like the English, you told me.'

'He's not so bad when you get to know him. Anyway, he's showing me a way up the other side of the hills. That's why I'm putting on my boots.' Bryn was surprised how easily the false story unfolded.

He quickly finished dressing, and left the house before he faced more questions.

Turning his face upwards, he felt the warming rays of the sun. *Must concentrate on where I climbed to find that cave. If I find it, and can get down again, how do I let Selwyn know? Didn't see a phone in his place.*

'Dreaming again?' said a familiar voice.

Bryn turned to see Idris padding along the path, with easy strides, to reach his side. Beads of sweat were glistening on his face, and his eyes shone with the satisfaction of hard exercise and fitness.

'Thinking about my tumble.'

'Heard about it. Thought you were a goat, did you?' Idris slowed to walk beside Bryn. 'What were you doing so far up the slopes?

'Cadno was chasing a rabbit.'

'White one, wasn't it? Strange that, a white rabbit in these parts.'

'How did you know?'

Idris smiled. 'Not much happens round here that I don't get to hear.' He began to jog on the spot. 'Must get on with my run.'

He trotted past Bryn and stopped some distance away, before turning round, and jogging backwards.

'Strange day, isn't it? Not a breath of wind. So still, you can feel the tension in the air. It's as if something important is waiting to happen, don't you think?'

Bryn could only nod his head and watch the strange Idris wave, then race round the corner and disappear.

The sky was clear except for some fluffy clouds over the hills. As he watched, Bryn saw the clouds over the peaks clump together, and thicken, forming a familiar shape. He clenched his fists as a horse's head was formed for a moment, then it disappeared.

Now to find the way up, thought Bryn, and walked until he reached the path ascending the hill. He climbed, then turned right to trace the path round the hill, and finally reached the altar-like stone.

Bryn shivered despite the sun. The hollow was becoming increasingly cold, and a strengthening breeze swirled round. He listened to the sighing of the breeze, and could imagine hearing familiar words.

Taking off his knapsack, he opened it, and extracted a pair of binoculars he had borrowed from his grandfather. He had told the old man that Idris was keen on bird watching, when asked the reason for the loan.

Must be somewhere up there, thought Bryn, swinging the glasses up the steep slope, as he stared through the lenses.

As he focussed the binoculars, the rocks, scrub, and scanty bushes leapt into sharp relief. It looked very hostile, and Bryn could see several sharp rocks protruding from the sparse grassy areas, waiting for the unwary to tumble down.

A rumble of thunder made him look up. The clouds at the peak of Court of Foxes were black, whereas the surrounding peaks were still bathed in sunshine. Bryn lowered his binoculars and listened to the thunder.

'Don't like this. Don't like this one little bit,' he said aloud. 'Not sure I want to go on.'

As he contemplated what to do, Bryn leaned against the wizard's rock and let his thoughts dwell on recent events. He was unaware of the developing mist behind him. Wisps of light grey writhed their way from the wizard's stone down the hill, thickening as they descended. The thin mist spread along the slopes, and joined to form an increasingly thick blanket until the lower part of the hill was hidden from view.

Bryn felt a tug on his anorak collar and turned his head. Tingles ran down his back as he looked at the white rabbit sitting on the rock, casually washing its face. He could see the mist, now a thick blanket of fog, blocking his way back. There were only two options left, to stay by the rock or climb up the slopes.

The fog rolled upwards, reached the stone, and spilled over the top, to writhe round his ankles.

'Mum!' cried Bryn, as terror overcame his senses. This was becoming a repetition of the momentous day when the secret cave had revealed its secret.

He clenched his fists and closed his eyes tightly to stop the tears welling inside. The moaning of the wind eased. His breathing slowed to normal and his heart ceased trying to batter its way out of his chest.

Bryn opened his eyes and pushed himself off the wizard's stone. The fog bank had stopped rolling forwards. A shaft of sunlight pierced the gloom of the black clouds at the summit, bathing the slope in a beam of light, illuminating the way ahead.

His hands were still trembling as he focussed the binoculars on the hill, and slowly scanned the view as he moved the glasses from side to side and upwards.

Scrub, grey rocks, loose stones, patches of grass, and bushes were scrutinised closely, but there was no sign of the solitary tree.

Bryn saw the top of the hill and moving the binoculars to the right, stopped, and turned the focussing ring. It was there. The tree, with its familiar knarled shape stood out against the rocks.

Did I really climb up that high? Bryn thought. He noticed the rabbit had hopped in front and was staring up at him.

'You want me to follow you, I suppose.'

The rabbit did a final grooming of its whiskers, ran up the hill for a few metres, stopped, and looked down at Bryn.

Placing the binoculars back in his knapsack, Bryn put his arms through the straps, and hitched the bag on his back. He looked past the rabbit and up the hill. It was going to be a long hard climb.

He was glad he was wearing boots as his feet crunched over the stones littering the ground. There was a path, of sorts, winding its way round and up the hill. Walking became harder as the incline of the slope increased, and the path disappeared. Soon Bryn was scrambling over outcrops of rocks, grabbing the sparse bushes for support. Occasionally he slipped, sending stones hurtling downwards, but did not dare look down.

Must only look upwards at the tree. Hate heights. Always did. The tree looks as far away as before. How long must I climb? My legs are aching now. In fact all of me is aching.

When the rocky face became more vertical, Bryn found

he had to lean down and use his hands to grip the ground to help him climb.

He yelled as he slipped, fell onto his stomach, and began to slide downwards, hands clutching at the ground. His tumble was broken by a thorn bush which scratched his hands.

Blood oozed from numerous cuts. The muscles in his right thigh throbbed, and the ankle hurt when he tried to stand up.

What do I do now, he thought, wincing as he put some weight on his injured foot.

The rabbit had hopped down the hillside, and sat on its haunches, watching, knowing he would not abandon the climb.

'Let's go,' said Bryn, and focussed on the tree as he slowly moved away from the bush. Each step was hard, and hot pain shot up his leg each time his right foot touched the ground.

He had no idea how long he climbed, and to relieve the throbbing in his foot, Bryn went down on hands and knees. Then he was at journey's end. His tired eyes were fixed on the tree, now within his grasp.

An arm was extended, and the course bark touched, then a final push from both feet had him standing upright. He clasped the trunk with both arms. Looking down, he could see no trace of the fog. The hillside down to the wizard stone and beyond was clear.

Bryn shaded his eyes with one hand as a bright flash from near the stream temporarily blinded him. The sun was bouncing off something reflective.

He squinted to try and see clearer, and began to ease his rucksack off. His feet slipped, and he was forced to abandon the move, and clutch the tree again.

As he eased his way round to the cave opening, the flashing light had gone. Bryn entered the cave, and stopped to retrieve a torch from his bag. The beam played round the damp wall and glistening stalactites, as he concentrated on carefully placing his injured foot down.

Painfully, he went down the slope, and used his free hand to steady himself on the cold rocky wall. It was becoming increasingly cold, and Bryn was glad he'd had the foresight to bring a torch. There was no blue light in the cave this time, not even when he turned the final corner to reach the chamber.

But the book of seven locks was bathed in blue light, radiating from the smooth leather cover, which pulsated with a life of its own.

Bryn winced as he hobbled towards the stone slab, his eyes fixed on the book. It looked sinister, glowing in the blue haze. The cold of the cave made his breath leave his nostrils like jets of steam, and his heart raced with a strange excitement.

He looked round, half expecting to see a black fox, or-even worse- the ghost of Emrys Morgan. No other being, human or animal, was keeping him company, only his imagination.

Standing by the slab, Bryn stared at the book, and slowly extended an arm. His fingers gently touched the leather, and he tensed, waiting for the surge of the supernatural force up his arm.

Nothing happened, except the leather rippled in waves, which increased as Bryn caressed the cover. It was just like a cat arching its back with pleasure when stroked.

Don't want to stay here longer than necessary, thought Bryn, undoing his knapsack. This place gives me the creeps.

He carefully lifted the book and eased it into his bag, followed by the keys, then replaced the bag on his back, adjusting the straps. Looking round the cave one more time, he retraced his steps up the narrow corridor to the entrance.

The sun was still blazing in a clear blue sky, and the black clouds had gone. Only fluffy white clouds crowned the peaks of the Court of Foxes as Bryn gazed round. There appeared to be a semblance of a path leading from the entrance to his right. It ran across the face of the hill then disappeared round a prominent jagged rock.

'Why didn't you show me this on the way up?' said Bryn, seeing the rabbit hopping into view.

He hitched the bag into a more comfortable position on his shoulders. The book was heavier than he had imagined. Carefully, he stepped off the ledge and onto the path.

Casually glancing downwards, he cried out and shut his eyes as a blinding flash of light reached towards him from the ground. He recoiled against the hillside as the meaning of the flashing light sunk in.

Someone was by the stream with a pair of binoculars. The sunlight, reflecting off the lenses, betrayed the watcher's position. He had been tracked as he climbed the hill to the secret cave.

Selwyn's last words intruded into his thoughts, as he pondered his next move.

'You must be mindful that if I know you have discovered the secret book, then others will have their suspicions. Be on your guard.'

CHAPTER TWENTY-TWO

Bryn struggled along the hillside, the path petering out, leaving him scrabbling over rocky outcrops clinging to the jagged surfaces. He dared not look down, and tried not to think about the watcher far below. His concentration was needed to make painful slow progress round the hillside, and find a way down to safety.

He shivered as the first drops of rain hissed down. A rumble of thunder made him look up. The peaks were hidden by, angry looking thick black clouds. He was in for a very wet journey, before reaching safety, and taking the book to Selwyn.

Wonder what he'll do with it, thought Bryn, inching his way along. The book was heavy as it bumped along his back. His heart lurched as one foot slipped, sending flakes of rocks tumbling down the hillside.

He looked ahead to see the rock face overhanging his way forward. The rain was heavier, and water streamed down his face.

'Wish I was home,' he cried, then pictured the wise old

face of Selwyn. He tried to imagine the old man waiting round the corner, smiling, and urging him on.

Bryn reached the overhang, and found the only way to progress was lie on his stomach and inch forwards.

It seemed hours before he was clear and could stand again. In front of him a path led down, and he gingerly walked across and began the descent.

Gradually the rain ceased, and the sun fought to break through the clouds. Bryn began to stride out as his feet trod on firmer ground. His spirits lifted as he saw the wood on the other side of the stream. It was to his left, which meant he was not going to be far from the crossing.

The sun warmed him, and as he walked, steam began to rise from his clothes. Not long now, he thought. Cross the stream, through the trees, then the welcome sight of Selwyn's cottage.

He hitched the rucksack on his back, his shoulders sore from the tight straps. Finally he stood on the streamside path.

'Caught out in the rain, I see.'

Bryn turned to see the rotund figure of Hugh Price, dressed in a dark blue anorak, pedalling with difficulty. His bicycle wobbled as he steered through the puddles of water.

'What are you doing out here, sir?'

'I've been indulging in my passion for wild bird life. It's called Ornithology, by the way.' Hugh dismounted, and patted the binoculars, which hung round his neck.

'And what is your reason for being out in such weather?'

'I've been climbing with Idris. He knows these hills like the back of his hand. I was on my way home when the rain came.' Bryn grimaced. 'I got soaked.'

The teacher stared at him, a fixed smile on his face. He pointed at the rucksack.

'And what are you carrying?'

'Some sandwiches, and a.... flask of tea,' said Bryn, racking his brains for a plausible explanation.

'Were you anywhere near where you became lost in that…fog I believe, the other day?'

'That was miles away, sir.'

'I see,' said Hugh, mounting his cycle. 'Must leave you now, and try and sight where some interesting birds are nesting. And I suggest you make haste home, and get out of those sodden clothes.' He cycled past Bryn, who watched him gradually recede into the distance, then disappear as the path curved round the hill.

Bryn waited a few minutes to ensure the teacher did not change his mind, then walked back to the crossing. Carefully picking his way across the stones, he reached the other bank then walked briskly towards the trees.

He found it an increasing effort to walk, yet he knew he must not stop. He just wanted to lie down and go to sleep. It was a fight to keep his eyes open, and focus on progress through the wood. The book was a dead weight, bumping on his back. He cried out as his feet caught in an exposed tree root, and he tumbled to the ground.

'Dear, dear. What a travesty of a well dressed boy you are,' said Selwyn. He extended a strong hand, and grasping Bryn's arm, pulled him to his feet.

'What did you say?' mumbled Bryn, brushing fallen leaves off his clothes.

'I said you were a travesty, but in simplistic terms, you look a mess.' Selwyn leaned on his staff and shook his head.

'Tut, tut, Bryn. What will you mother say when she sees you have torn your clothes again?'

'Kill me, I suppose,' said Bryn, as he followed the old man out of the trees.

Selwyn, turned his head and smiled. 'Let us hope she does not resort to such extreme measures in her chastisement of you.'

Bryn grinned back. 'I haven't a clue what you mean, but I'm sure you're right.'

He hitched his rucksack, and winced. The skin felt tender under his shirt. It would be wonderful relief to reach the cottage, and get the weight off his back.

'Selwyn, how did you know I was coming? You weren't here by accident, were you?'

'Very perceptive, Bryn,' said the old man. 'Another of my young friends informed me, and…'

'Idris?'

'Indeed. He may seem strange to many in the village, but he knows much. His mind tunes into the forces that abound here. I have been watching your progress on the hills from my cottage, with my telescope.'

'Does he know about Emrys Morgan and the book of seven locks?'

Selwyn nodded, and quickened his pace as they exited the trees. His cottage was a welcome sight, with smoke curling upwards from the chimney.

As he pushed open the door, Selwyn smiled at Bryn, and placed a friendly hand on his shoulders.

'Idris knew you were special the first time he met you. He told me that he experienced a great force emanating from your persona.'

'Selwyn,' said Bryn, entering the cottage and easing his rucksack off his aching shoulders. 'I wish you'd talk to me so that I can understand.'

'Simplistic terms?'

'Whatever.'

'Idris was frightened when he first met you. That is why he tried to cover it up by being so…hostile. It was me who told him to get to know you better. Find out what makes you…tick, I believe is the word.'

'Idris frightened of me?' Bryn walked to the sink, filled the kettle, and placed it on the stove. 'I thought he hated me, just because I was born in England.' He turned to Selwyn.

'Carys and the others don't like him much, do they? I know he isn't in their secret club.'

'Carys also picks up signals, like Idris. She is aware that he does not think about the malevolent life forces in the village like her. As I have said before, Bryn, this village has been divided into two for over a hundred years. There were those who believed in the Black Fox, and his powers. And the others, who would publically say it was all a nonsense, but secretly were afraid.'

Selwyn walked to a cupboard, pulled open the top drawer, and retrieved some contents. Filling a small bowl with hot water from a tap, he wandered over to Bryn, and indicated he should sit down.

'Now, let's clean up that mess before you go home. You mother will not exactly praise you, young Bryn, when she sees your clothes.'

Bryn winced as Selwyn carefully washed the torn skin on his legs and hands. After drying the wounds gently with lint, the old man uncrewed a small jar. It contained an orange coloured paste, which Selwyn eased out with the back of a spoon. Bryn felt instant relief as the paste was liberally applied to his wounds.

'That's amazing,' said Bryn, relaxing into the chair. 'The pain has gone, just like magic.'

'Magic maybe, but certainly not the magic of Emrys Morgan. In fact it is one of several potions I have learned to make over the years. But now to business.'

Selwyn walked over to the rucksack, picked it up, and placed it on his table. Bryn could see his hands were trembling as he undid the cover, then sat down in a chair.

He sighed as the leather-bound volume was eased out,

and grasped firmly in one hand, while the other caressed the smooth leather.

'A scroll with writing on both sides and sealed with seven seals,' whispered Selwyn. He fingered the small gold locks, and turned to Bryn.

'You have the keys?'

'In the rucksack.'

A beam of sunshine poured through the window, and struck the book, making the leather gleam. Bryn watched as the leather began to pulsate with an inner energy. He had seen the book undulate before in the cave, and for some reason, he was frightened again.

'Don't like it, Selwyn,' he cried. 'I've seen it do that in the cave.'

'Then there is no time to be lost,' said Selwyn. 'The Black Fox wants his inheritance and wreak havoc.'

The sunbeam vanished, just as if someone had flicked a switch. Outside, the sun was obscured by cloud. The wind rose in strength, until the windows were rattling.

Selwyn knew that this was not a sudden freak of climate. Something was announcing its prescence and power. The book writhed and twisted in an effort to escape his clutches.

'What's happening,' cried Bryn, as windows shattered and the wind screamed into the room, scattering books, and smashing crockery to the floor.

Selwyn struggled to hold the book, which wriggled out of his hands, and slid away from his grasp along the table. It upended, so that the locks were tantalisingly close. The old man was pinned to his chair, his hair streaming behind him. He gasped, and tried to force himself forwards to reach the book, but the gale raged out of control.

'I fear we have been overtaken by Satans' forces, and I must summon help.' He closed his eyes and concentrated on his words.

'In the name of the Supreme Goodness, I command…'

His words were muffled by a towel, which flew across the room and wrapped itself round his mouth.

'Selwyn!' yelled Bryn, and tried to stand up. The gale in the room slammed him back. He was pinnioned as securely as if someone had tied him to the chair.

As suddenly as it came, the wind ceased. The silence that followed was ominous. Bryn found himself staring at the door, terrified and shivering. Tears trickled down his face as he waited for something to happen.

The door burst open, and a figure stood in the entrance, menacing and purposeful. Four ghostly foxes padded into the room, trotted up to Bryn, and sat down by his feet. They gazed up at him with sinister red eyes.

CHAPTER TWENTY-THREE

The son of sons of Cadno Du has finally shown us the true resting place of the sacred book.' Hugh Price strode into the room followed by several other men from the village. He walked to the book and bowed in supplication. The other men followed his example, then Hugh carefully picked up the volume and kissed the leather.

Turning round, he lifted the book above his head, and beads of sweat stood out on his forehead. His eyes burned with excitement and his voice shook, as he spoke to his followers.

'Who will not fear you, O Lord, and bring glory to your name?' Hugh looked at Selwyn and Bryn. 'Only the true believers know that those words relate to the Great Dragon, Satan himself. We always knew the sacred book was here in Morredin, but where?

'For generations, his disciples searched and searched so that the Black Fox could come back to us, and…'

'Back?' whispered Bryn.

'Why should your Christ be the only person able to be

resurrected? You, Bryn, know better than any of us the power of Emrys Morgan. You have heard him, felt his prescence, haven't you?'

Bryn nodded and stared at the floor. He could not argue with his teacher about events that had taken over his life since living in the village.

How can I forget that first time when I felt I was not alone, running by the stream? Was it just imagination when I felt someone near me at school? And seeing dad at the match. Only it wasn't him. And then there are the foxes.

He pointed to the four animals by his feet. 'Can you see them?'

'See what?

'Those foxes sitting there.'

'No, Bryn. I cannot see foxes because I am not of the Black Fox family line. Only the true descendants have those powers.' Hugh smiled. 'We quickly learned of your visions, which only confirmed what we had suspected.'

Hugh brought the book near Bryn. 'Within these pages are the secrets of our King, the Lord Satan, the Great Dragon. When Emrys Morgan is restored, he will summon the rightful inheritor of the Universe. You will see real power over all life.'

The teacher clicked his fingers and pointed to Selwyn, who had taken the towel off his face. He opened his mouth to repeat the incantation to the Supreme Goodness.

One of the men snatched the towel, twisting it into a thick band. Forcing it into the old man's mouth, the man looped ends round the back of his neck, and tied it tightly.

Selwyn tried to remove the gag, but was restrained by another man who produced some rope and swiftly tied him to the chair.

'That will keep you quiet, old man. You have been enough trouble over the years,' said Hugh, walking forwards and looking down into Selwyn's eyes, which blazed with fury.

'And you, Bryn,' said the teacher, turning round, 'The power of Emrys Morgan courses strongly in your blood. You can take his mantle and stand by his side when he returns. You will have powers unheard of.' Hugh's eyes softened momentarily. 'I know I have been regarded as a joke at school and in the village. Oh yes, I am aware of my name. "Farty Hugh", isn't it?'

My parents worshipped the Great Dragon, and their parents before them. When I learned of the stories surrounding Emrys Morgan all those years ago, I knew where I had to journey. And the rest, as they say, is history.' He chuckled, 'In fact I'm a pretty good teacher.'

Bryn stared at him, his mind a jumble. How could this fat, bumbling man, who sweated freely, farted frequently, be someone so frightening? The book was a reality, but could it really have secrets contained within its pages that could change everything?

And who am I? Before I came to Morredin, I was just Bryn Mitchell who played football pretty well, and hoped to join the Rams one day. I had my mates, and went to school, though I hated it. Now I am being told I'm related to a monster, who can have his photo taken when he's dead.

'Not sure what you want, sir,' said Bryn, still giving Hugh the respect of his profession.

'Want?' said Hugh. 'What I want is to finish the great work of Emrys Morgan, and you can help, if you have the desire.' He stood over Bryn and held the book close to his face.

'Today will be the climax of everything. The world will change forever, and you can take your rightful place by the Great Dragon. He will reward those who have served him.' His voice rose excitedly, and he kissed the book. 'Armageddon will come as prophesised in the Revelations. Cities will be destroyed, earthquakes will sink islands, and hailstones like huge boulders will hurtle out of the sky. Then the world will kneel before the true King.' He rocked on his heels with fervour, and the sweat poured down his face.

'What if I don't want to?' said Bryn, the smell of the sweaty body of the teacher overwhelming.

'That is for you to decide, Bryn. We have the capacity to make up our own minds. That is a human frailty in my opinion, which will alter when the new order takes over. In any case, your work is done. The book could not come back to life until the power of the Black Fox flowed back into its pages.' He stroked the book. 'And you did that for him by touching it.'

A man came forwards and tied Bryn in his chair, as the foxes slunk out of the cottage.

'We will leave you now and begin our historic duty to summon Emrys Morgan, and our King.' Hugh walked to the door, and motioned to one of the men to collect the keys.

At the doorway, he turned round. 'One more thing, Bryn. You will have the chance to be free and join us, if you listen to your inner voice. The supreme power of the Great Dragon has been shown. Who else can change the weather from sun to thunder and hailstones, just in Morredin? Freeing you from your bonds will be easy for my master.'

'Will someone…or something come?' whispered Bryn.

'That will be your surprise,' said Hugh, and strode out of the cottage, slamming the door shut.

Bryn sat in his chair, terrified at what might happen. He could not take his eyes away from the door, wondering what might enter. Only the ticking of the wall clock disturbed the silence.

Selwyn had his back to him, and Bryn could see the old man struggling to free himself, but the bonds were too tight. Steam poured from the kettle indicating the water was boiling, ready to fill the two mugs on the table.

Could do with a cup of tea, thought Bryn, licking his dry

lips. Wouldn't mind something to eat either. What happens now?

He thought about the last words of the teacher and people having choices. What sort of power does old Farty think I have, being related to Emrys Morgan?

'Seem to have made a mess of things, Selwyn,' said Bryn, receiving a series of grunts from the old man in reply.

Tick, tock, was the only sound in the room, and Bryn stared at the clock, whilst trying to collect his thoughts.

He glanced up and was aware of the light rapidly fading outside, though still early afternoon. A light mist wafted through the broken windows, carrying a smell Bryn recognised. He shuddered as he recalled his nightmares again. This was the smell of the grave, of rotting corpses. This was the smell of evil yet to come.

The effort of climbing back to the cave, and retrieving the book, overcame him. Bryn found himself nodding, and jerked his head upright again to stop himself dozing. His eyes were leaden, and as fatigue overcame his resistance, his head dropped down and sleep came in waves.

The click of the latch brought Bryn back to consciousness. His eyes snapped open, and he watched the creaking door slowly open. Aware of his heart slamming madly in his chest, he could only stare with increasing terror until the door was fully open. He waited for the thing from hell to enter.

'Well, well. Not a pretty sight, is it?' said Idris, walking into the room.

'You?' said Bryn.

'Who were you expecting?' said Idris, and walked towards the heaving body of Selwyn. Quickly untying the gag, he then turned his attention to the bonds.

'Dunno. Something horrible though,' said Bryn.

'Thanks for the compliment. Been called worse and…'

'No time, Idris. No time for chit-chat,' whispered Selwyn,

and gestured to the sink. Idris quickly filled a glass with water and brought it back.

Selwyn drained the glass, and leaned back in the chair. He coughed noisily, then closed his eyes and took a few deep breaths.

'That's better. Now untie Bryn. He has decisions to make, as to his involvement in these events, before this day is over.'

Idris struggled to untie the knots on the rope restraining Bryn, and swore repeatedly. Finally the rope dropped to the floor, and Bryn stood up, gingerly stretching his legs.

'Thanks, Idris, for not being the horrible thing I was expecting.' Bryn grinned at the taller boy, who smiled briefly, and gave a playful punch back in reply.

'Bryn, come here,' said Selwyn, coughing again. He lifted the gold necklace off his neck, and placed it on the table. Standing up, his trembling hands stroked the gold chain.

'When you leave this cottage, you leave the protection of the Supreme Goodness.'

'Then I won't go,' said Bryn.

'You have to. It is your destiny. Kismet, fate, call it what you will, Bryn. It is my belief you were always going to come here. If you remember, I said you were here for a purpose when we first met. Only then, I could not perceive the reason.' Selwyn's voice trembled. 'Hugh Price was correct when he said you had to listen to your inner self. You must leave here and proceed to where they are assembled. You will then take certain action over which neither Hugh nor I, have control. He believes that as the son of sons of Cadno Du, you will embrace him and help his return to this world.'

The old man picked up the necklace and placed it round Bryn's neck. His fingers held up the small ornament at the end.

'What nobody knows is that there is an eighth key to the

book, which can bring down such a power of destruction.'

'On us?'

'No, Bryn, but on the book and its contents. I was given it many years ago by a holy man I met on my travels. He was dying, and when he knew I was coming here to search for the book of seven keys, he entrusted me with this precious gift. I do not know how he came by the key, but it is lucky for mankind he had it. Sadly he died before he was prepared to impart to me how the key came into his posession, but he knew its purpose.' Selwyn smiled. 'You see, even your forebears were aware that if the secrets fell into the wrong hands, then the great plan would be in danger. Better to destroy the book than incur the wrath of Satan.'

'Do I just turn the key?'

'I wish it were that simple. No, Bryn, there are sacred words to say.'

'What words?'

'Sadly, that is my predicament.' Selwyn cupped Bryn's face and spoke quietly. 'I can teach you the words, but only you can decide if they are used.'

Bryn stared at the old man, seeing the concern in his eyes, and looked at Idris, who was pouring hot water into the two mugs.

'What should I do, Idris?'

'Not my problem, see,' said Idris, shrugging his shoulders. He placed the kettle back on the stove. 'But I think you should do as Selwyn wants.'

'It's your decision, Bryn,' croaked Selwyn.

'I'll go then.'

'Good,' said Selwyn, and beamed with happiness. 'Idris will go with you.' Seeing the shocked expression in the older boy's face, Selwyn expressed his concern.

'Bryn will need your support and company. He is embarking on a journey fraught with danger, and needs friends. I know I can rely on you, Idris. Now let us prepare.'

Bryn sipped his tea and listened intently as Selwyn slowly repeated the words needed before the key was used. He was made to say the incantation, over and over, until Selwyn was satisfied.

The wind increased in strength, and howled its anger as the two boys stepped outside the cottage. Thunder rumbled overhead in the blackening sky, and lightning crackled over the peaks of the Court of Foxes. There was an atmosphere of time standing still, waiting for momentous events.

'I shall pray for you both,' said Selwyn, clutching the door, his hair in disarray from the buffeting wind. 'When you leave here, Bryn, you will be tempted by Satan's forces to yield yourself to his will. I cannot guide you in this matter, neither can Idris. Do not imagine it will be easy.'

He hugged Bryn closely, then gently pushed him away, saying, 'May the Supreme Goodness be with you.'

Waving goodbye, Bryn walked down the path with Idris. Neither boy looked at each other, immersed in their own thoughts.

Bryn tried to ignore the pack of ghostly foxes that trotted on each side of the path. As they made their way to the wood, Bryn could see other animals waiting in the trees, their red eyes blazing in the increasing gloom. Silently, they would leave their cover and join the pack.

Soon dozens of foxes were slipping through the trees, forming an escort on each side of the boys.

Bryn cried out and clapped his hands to his ears as a familiar voice intruded into his mind.

'See how my followers from another time escort you, Bryn, the son of sons of Cadno Do. Are you not proud to be so revered? Soon I will join you, and we will be renuited, embracing each other, as father and son. For I am your real father, Bryn, not that bumbling, drink-ridden apology you lived with. Surely you realise that?'

'Don't want to listen,' cried Bryn, sinking to his knees.

'What's the matter?' said Idris, rushing forwards, then stopped. The ghostly foxes became visible as they formed a protective circle round Bryn. They turned their heads to look at Idris, hatred in their eyes, and lips curled back to reveal large white fangs.

'Where…where did they come from?' he whispered.

'Can you see them?' said Bryn, pointing to the foxes sitting on their haunches.

Idris nodded. 'One minute you were on your own, the next minute surrounded by them.'

'They've been with us all the time. I've been seeing them for ages.' Bryn sighed, and stood up. 'It's to do with me being related to Emrys Morgan.' He walked out of the circle, the animals moving to one side, and listened. Only the wind moaning through the swaying, creaking trees disturbed the silence.

'Better move on,' said Bryn, 'though I wonder why you can now see the foxes. Don't like it.'

'Not so happy myself. They don't look friendly,' said Idris seeing the animals still baring their fangs at him.

'They won't hurt you, 'cos they are here for me. Sort of escort, I think, sent by Emrys.' Bryn looked at Idris. 'I don't know who I am any longer. That's the trouble. I came here as Bryn Mitchell, now voices tell me I am someone evil. Well, someone who has the power to be horrible.'

'You're a good person, see? But you have to go on, Bryn. I have seen things others haven't, but only Selwyn knows. He calls it "second sight".'

'Then what's going to happen?'

'Don't know, Bryn. Wish I did.'

The boys pushed on through the trees until they could see

the stream, glistening in the dim light. Bryn shuddered as he looked at the tumbling water. It was coloured blood red, but was now hurtling through the fields at immense speed. Foam was thrown upwards, in a red curtain. He remembered when the sky had been red, followed by a deluge of real blood. That had been in a dream, or had he really experienced the horror whilst out on the hills? He was finding it difficult to separate reality from fantasy.

A gentle breeze replaced the howling wind as they walked across the crossing stones, followed by the foxes gliding over the water. No splashes surrounded the numerous feet paddling across, the water continuing to pour downstream, undisturbed.

'That's weird,' said Idris as he watched their animal escort ford the stream.

'But they're not from our world, are they?' said Bryn. He looked ahead, and pointed. 'I think the ghosts of all the foxes who ever lived here are waiting for us.'

On the other side of the stream, dozens of the animals stood, waiting for the boys. The foxes carpetted the hillside, their eyes shining like red beacons in the gloom.

As they watched, the boys saw the mass of animals on the hill part to let a lone fox trot down towards them.

Bryn gasped as he looked at the animal, much larger and muscular than its brothers. Even in the gloom, it was easy to pick out the glossy, jet-black coat.

'It's Cadno Du,' whispered Bryn. He watched it descend the hill, expecting a change into Emrys Morgan any moment.

CHAPTER TWENTY-FOUR

The fox sat a few feet from the boys, lifted its huge head, and stared at Bryn, its red eyes blazing with passion. He could not resist the creature's gaze, and heard its words in his mind, though nothing was audible.

'You have seen the power of our King, and through me, you have power unheard of by mankind. Look at the stream, Bryn, and make the water flow the other way.'

'That's impossible,' said Bryn, turning to look at the fast running water.

'What's impossible?' asked Idris.

'Making the stream go the other way.'

'Who said you could?'

'The fox, or is it Emrys Morgan?'

'Do as I say, Bryn,' said the fox. 'You can make the water stop, then go backwards, You are the son of sons, and that gives you power even over nature.'

The fox reared up on its back legs, baring frightening yellow gangs. Bryn heard just two words hammering into his mind.

'Do it!'

He turned round and gazed at the bubbling stream. It was dashing along at increasing speed, pink froth forming where the rocks and stones impeded its progress.

How can I make it go the other way? This is crazy.

'Do it!' commanded the voice.

Bryn took a deep breath, and stared at the stream. He frowned as he concentrated on reversing the flow. As he focussed his thoughts, he sensed a powerful energy well inside his body, then pour out over the water. He swayed slightly, as he concentrated. Even the sound of the rushing stream was erased from his mind, as his body trembled with the surge of power.

Idris stared, with disbelieving eyes, as the water slowed, then stopped. It resumed its journey in the opposite direction. Bryn had made the impossible happen.

Coming out of his trance-like state, Bryn watched the stream bubbling its way past him then continue its journey up the hill. He was weak with the effort, and his legs were like jelly.

'Did I really do that?' he whispered, collapsing on the ground, frail but excited at his miracle-like achievment.

'Just think what more you can do when I come back, and the Great Dragon takes his rightful inheritance, Bryn. Together, you and I will have such powers over the Universe. We will be such a team, that the world will tremble before us.'

Bryn listened to the unspoken words of Cadno Du thundering in his head, and hearing an increasing noise from the sky.

Thunder sounded like the hooves of galloping horses, as the clouds parted and revealed a brilliant red sky. Crimson-coloured horses hurtled past, manes and tails streaming.

Steam pouring from flared nostrils, and eyes blazing with evil.

Idris looked up at the sinister spectacle, and cried out as a pale horse brought up the rear, with a black-cloaked rider. Bryn had seen that horse before, and knew the identity of the rider. He was surprised when the skeletal figure raised his scythe in salute as he passed, then bowed deeply in supplication.

'What's happening?' cried Idris, and began to move towards Bryn. The foxes moved silently to confront him, forming a barrier.

'I'm going on,' said Bryn. 'I have to, Idris. It's my destiny.' He looked at the increasing numbers of foxes now surrounding his friend. 'You can't come with me. Cadno Du says so.'

'I must,' said Idris, hesitating to move. 'Selwyn sent me to protect you.'

The foxes glared at Idris, and bared their fangs in a show of antagonism, daring him to move. He was unsure of what these ghostly animals were capable of. Could they really attack him and rip him to pieces?

'Tell the foxes to let me through, Bryn. You must have power over them.'

Bryn shook his head, and pointed to the black fox now sitting by his side.

'Don't you understand? Cadno Du is the King of foxes here. When Emrys Morgan, who could change into a fox, died, all the foxes left to form other packs, I imagine everywhere in Wales and probably England. Why do you think this hill is called Court of Foxes?'

Idris was worried as he looked at his friend. His eyes were wide and shining. His face glowed with excitement at what he had done, and the promise of future power. Selwyn had told Bryn it was up to him what path he took. It was all about choices. Was Bryn going to make the wrong choice that would mean disaster for the world, and evil, such as no one had ever known, in control?

'Bryn, remember what Selwyn told you.'

'He's just a stupid old fool. Just look at the stream going the wrong way. That's just for starters. I could do anything… such as…be the best player the Rams have ever seen. Just imagine that?'

Bryn stretched out his arms to the pulsating red sky and screamed, 'I am the son of the sons of Cadno Du.'

The black fox walked slowly to the animals encircling Idris. They parted to let their leader face him. It stared at Idris for a moment, its malevolent gaze making him shiver with fear.

He could not stop himself looking into the two red eyes, glowing with evil. At that moment Idris knew that despite having powers of second sight, he was facing a force mankind had flirted with over the ages. Wars, genocides, everyday murders and atrocities, were just a taste of horrors to come if the Great Dragon, Satan, was to rule the Universe.

'Bryn, stop and think. I beg you, before you release something you will regret for always.'

Growls from the foxes round him, reinforced by a baring of teeth, stopped Idris from following. Bryn turned his back and continued along the path, accompanied by the black fox.

Monstrous creatures from hell were cavorting in the sky, and the black–cloaked figure of Death continued to wheel round the crimson clouds.

Idris sank to his knees, and cried out in his fear. Tears tumbled down the face of a youth, known for his toughness, now terrified for the future. He called out for help to someone he had previously mocked.

'God, please help us.'

Bryn followed the black fox along the winding path that gradually climbed the hill. The eerie light made everything a crimson colour. Grass, pebbles, bushes, trees were transformed into varying hues of red. The light breeze ruffling the long grass in the hollows gave the impression of it being on fire.

The hordes from the Netherworld continued their macabre dance in the sky over Bryn and his fox companion. As they progressed round the hill, and upwards, the massed ranks of the other animals parted. They watched closely, saliva drooling from their jaws. And all the time there were the screams from hell saying over and over again, 'Adentium, Adentium'.

Finally Bryn turned a corner and reached the site of Craig y Dewin, the Wizard's Rock. It was glowing in a beacon, shining down from the sky. The light pulsated, playing over the rock, giving the impression the stone shimmered with a life of its own.

In the centre of the altar lay the book of seven locks, the keys detached from the ring. Hugh knelt down, and kissed the stone, then stood and reverantly picked up the book. He held it close to himself, and closed his eyes, swaying as he was overcome by the emotion of the occasion.

He was wearing a black monk-like cloak, and had painted black stripes down his face and across the bald patch on the top of his head.

Bryn gazed at the group behind Hugh on the hillside. He recognised many adults from the village with their children, then looked for Carys and Gwyn. They were standing with their parents, Carys fidgetting with excitement, whereas Gwyn looked terrified.

Bryn frowned, as the one person he expected to be present was absent. If anyone was like a witch and capable of casting spells, then Anwen Hughes fitted the description.

'Let us begin the solemn ceremony to bring our King, the Great Dragon to earth and claim his rightful inheritance,' said Hugh, and picked up one of the keys, which he inserted in the first lock and turned. The audible 'click' was heard by everyone on the hill, and a few cried with the enormity of the occasion.

'Adentium, mesantium,' intoned Hugh, and inserted the second key, then turned his head to smile at Bryn. 'I knew you would come, son of sons. Our master needs your help to come back.' He pointed at the black fox, and his voice quivered.

'See, how he becomes what he was in Morredin.'

Bryn's hairs on the nape of his neck became erect, and his heart hammered as his eyes followed Hugh's extended arm.

The black fox grew in size, and gradually changed shape, becoming human in form. Still ghostly in substance, Emrys Morgan stood in his Victorian finery and spoke to Hugh.

'Continue, good servant, and bridge the gap between time, space and eternity. Continue to preach from the sacred book and release its powers to bring the highest authority in the Universe here.'

He turned to Bryn, and his voice softened. He extended his arms and spun round.

'Soon all this will be yours, son of sons. Even now, the people down in Morredin are praying to their God to deliver them, and save their souls. But they cannot stop Dyn Hysbis now his son has chosen to take the righteous path.'

He nodded to Hugh, who bowed, then picked up a third key and inserted it in the book. As he clicked the lock open, the hill shuddered as an ominous rumble could be heard deep in the bowels of the earth.

People screamed with terror as stones rattled down the hillside. Huge boulders were dislodged and tumbled down, bouncing in the air as they hit rocky outcrops. The noise increased, and Bryn looked down in horror as the path split in a zigzag line, smoke and flames shooting upwards from the gap.

As he fell, Bryn could see adults and children sent sprawling. Hugh remained on his feet, still intoning the prayers to bring Satan into his Universe. The ghostly form of Emrys Morgan was by his side. Bryn glanced at Carys. She was still on her feet, hair in disarray. Whereas those around her were terrified at the sudden earthquake, Carys was smiling and mouthing the same prayers as Hugh.

The whole of the hillside was now undulating, and the thunder reverberated and crashed in the sky. Bryn was deafened as he scrambled to his feet and ran along the path, jumping over the widening cracks.

Hugh turned and beckoned him, as Emrys walked down to meet Bryn, smiling, though his eyes remained cold and hard.

'Even now, Bryn, the earth is moving and splitting in the valleys,' said Emrys. 'Huge waves are thundering in from the ocean. See for yourself.' He pointed to a cloud where a picture was forming of the nearby coast.

Bryn's eyes widened with the horror at the scene. It was as if he was in the sky looking down. He could see a huge wave, miles out to sea, thundering towards the shore. People, unaware of the impending disaster, strolled over the sands.

'Soon all the towns and villages by the sea in this part of Wales will be swept away,' said Emrys, as the picture faded from the cloud. 'You will see the power of the true creator and destroyer very soon. For he is coming. Just a few more locks to open and the awesome power will be released. Power, Bryn, that you shall inherit.'

He turned and pointed to a lonely cottage some distance from them. 'See what I can summon.'

Bryn could only watch as huge hailstones, the size

of boulders, hurtled out of the sky and quickly reduced the cottage to a pile of stones and broken roof timbers. He recalled the words of Revelation 16 and the huge hailstones.

'And they cursed God on account of the plague of hail, because the plague was so terrible.'

'Come, Bryn, and open the last sacred lock,' said Emrys, pointing to the altar. 'See, our King is gradually coming through time to join us,' he continued, extending an arm skywards.

Bryn stumbled to the altar, and took the book from Hugh. The teacher was trembling as he watched the sky become brighter where Emrys pointed. Out of the crimson light a whirling mist tumbled, gradually becoming a recognisable shape.

'It's him,' whispered Hugh, and sank to his knees.

The mist reached the ground and was visible as a huge dragon with seven heads that looked everywhere as their long necks twisted and turned. Huge black eyes peered balefully at the crowd on the hillside, who were silenced at the enormity of the evil presence. Several tried to flee but were stopped by the massed ranks of the foxes, now visible to everyone, surrounding them.

Fire streamed out of the monster's nostrils, setting the grass alight, and when it opened its huge mouth, showing sword-like curved fangs, it bellowed its defiance.

'I see you are not afraid,' said Emrys, looking at Bryn. 'Not like those mere mortals over there.'

'Why should I be?' said Bryn, noticing that Carys was trembling, tears coursing down her face. 'Am I not the son of sons of Cadno Du? Haven't you told me I have a choice?'

Yes, thought Bryn, looking at Carys again. It was just a game to you and your friends. All that acting in the cave was fun, and you were the leader. But this is different now. The acting is over and Emrys Morgan is here, to help something terrible happen.

'You have made it then?' said Emrys, interrupting his thoughts.

'Yes,' said Bryn. 'I knew my destiny from the moment I left the old man's cottage.'

'Give him the key,' said Emrys, and stood aside as Bryn walked to the stone. Hugh, still shaking, held out the last of the golden keys, and watched his pupil touch it with his left hand momentarily, then shake his head.

'Don't need that one, sir,' said Bryn, taking the book. He glanced at the evolving dragon growing larger, the red scales glowing with heat. All the heads were looking at him, their malevolent eyes fixed on the book.

Hordes of creatures from hell surrounded the Great Dragon, some on the ground and others flying overhead. The noise from their screeches was bloodcurdling.

Bryn felt the smoothness of the leather, and turned the book so that the spine faced him. In the centre he could see a small keyhole and gingerly ran a finger over it.

'Time now, sir,' he said to Hugh, who nodded and stood back from the altar. Bryn saw Emrys staring at him, confusion showing in his dark eyes.

The book was vibrating violently in Bryn's hands as though aware that something disturbing was imminent.

'Mantonemous, evictidous…' intoned Bryn, as he opened his right hand to reveal the key Selwyn had given him.

'What is happening?' cried Hugh as he listened to alien words.

'Stop him!' said Emrys, as Bryn continued uttering the words taught by Selwyn.

As Hugh lumbered forwards, Bryn inserted the key, turned it, and cried out the final words of the incantation.

The Great Dragon bellowed its anger, and Emrys watched

in horror as the book writhed in Bryn's hands. Hugh threw himself at the boy and snatched the book away.

'I have it, I have it,' he said, sitting on the ground and holding up the book.

'It's too late,' cried Emrys, and glared at Bryn who had been sent sprawling by Hugh's attack.

'What do you mean, too late? I have the sacred book. We can open the final lock and rule the world.'

Hugh reached out to the altar and wheezed his way upright. The stone was red hot, and he snatched his hand away. His wild eyes changed from a triumphant look to worry, then terror as he looked upwards.

The clouds parted and a column of dazzling white light burst through to reach the area round the altar. Lightning crackled down the column to reach the ground, sparks sizzling from stones and boulders which were melted.

Hugh was transfixed, his fate sealed, as a huge bolt of lightning hurtled from the heavens, and smashed into him and the altar. Flames shot skywards from the ground concealing both man and stone.

No smell of burning betrayed what was happening in that inferno. As quickly as they had come, the flames vanished, as did the Great Dragon and his entourage.

Bryn was shivering and crying as he looked at the altar. The huge stone was split into two, and where Hugh Price had stood, there was only a pile of ash. No trace of the evil book was visible. The cracks in the path had vanished, the surface complete again.

Silence replaced the recent thunder of the hellish storm. The sky overhead was dazzling bright, the previous red colour replaced by clear blue with fluffy white clouds. Bryn watched in awe as the form of a magnificent white horse pranced out of the sky. Its rider was dressed in a white robe, and held a golden sword. Behind him came dozens of similar riders, the only difference being their leader wore a golden crown.

The riders rode across the sky, then wheeled in formation and descended until a few feet above Bryn. As they passed, all the riders saluted Bryn with their swords, and their leader smiled and mouthed, 'Well done.'

Daylight returned and birds commenced to sing their delight that normality had come back to the hillside. The ghostly foxes were gone now they had no leader and could not return.

Bryn ambled to the altar and stared at the stone. It lay in two pieces with a clean split down the middle. He glanced at the ash on the ground and shuddered at the remains of his teacher.

Fatigue overcame him, so much energy had been expended in the task destiny had decreed. He slumped down on the ground and watched the people hurrying away from the place where they had assembled in expectation of momentous events. Now they were hushed, silenced by the ferocity of the forces that had sent Emrys back to the Netherland.

Bryn saw them avert their gaze from his challenging eyes. The previous fervour of being present at the reincarnation of Emrys Morgan had gone. Now they were just ordinary villagers from Morredin, frightened that they had witnessed a power greater than even the Great Dragon.

Gwyn briefly smiled as he passed, whereas Carys, crying bitterely, ignored Bryn's attempt at communication.

'Suit yourself,' said Bryn quietly, and watched the crowd gradually disappear from sight as they rounded the hill on their way down.

He watched birds flying round, calling to each other revelling in the peace that had been restored to the hill.

Better get back, thought Bryn, and winced as he stood, feeling the bruises from the tumble. He breathed in the fresh air, and closed his eyes. Time seemed to have flown past, and the clash of Good and Evil by the altar was receding already in his memory.

Maybe that's what's meant to happen, or I'll have even worse nightmares than before. Do hope I don't dream about that horrible cave again.

Bryn stepped carefully round the ash by his feet, and began the long walk home.

Rounding the hill, he saw two familiar people walking up to meet him, and forced his aching legs to run.

'So you decided to choose righteousness in the end,' said Selwyn, and hugged Bryn closely.

'I thought you had decided to join them all, the way you were talking,' said Idris.

'Can't say I wasn't tempted, 'specially when I made the stream go backwards. That was amazing. So cool.' Bryn looked up at the old man. 'But I knew, in my heart, I couldn't join them. It was terrible, and when the Great Dragon began to appear, I've never been so frightened.'

Bryn told them the whole story as they descended the hill back to the stream, and shuddered as he recounted how Hugh Price met his end. Remembering the picture on the cloud, Bryn turned to Selwyn, and told him what he had seen.

'Have you heard anything about the giant wave Emrys sent to destroy the coast?'

Selwyn stopped walking. 'Yes, there was a report on the radio. It was a news flash warning of a sudden, massive wave hurtling towards the coast. It was about thirty miles long, and fifty feet high. They were talking about a 'Tsunami,' and telling everybody to get to high ground, well away from the coast.'

The old man stroked his beard and smiled. 'Then another report came soon afterwards, saying that, miraculously, the wave had vanished and the sea was calm again. So, what you have done here, today, stopped the evil intentions of Emrys Morgan.'

'So it's finished then,' said Bryn, feeling a huge burden had been lifted. 'I am free from him.'

'That is the truth of the matter, my young friend. The evil soul of Cadno Du has been sent back to hell for all eternity. You will never hear from him again, but there is one thing.'

'What's that?'

'All the powers he gave you will have left your body.' Selwyn smiled. 'Alas, you are just a normal, sometimes cheeky, football mad, very brave boy.'

'I'll settle for that,' said Bryn, grinning. 'As long as I can play for the Rams.'

'Was ash deposited on the altar where the book had been?' asked Selwyn.

'Strange that,' said Bryn. 'Not a trace, but I'm sure it was burned. You should have seen the flames and felt the heat.'

'I hope you're right, Bryn,' muttered Selwyn. 'If that book was, somehow, rescued, we're in trouble. I only had the one key.'

'Well you'd better have it back then,' laughed Bryn, and opened his hand.

SPRING

B ryn walked by the stream, eyes half closed, feeling the hot sun on his face. He tingled with excitement as he recalled the match the previous day.

The third team of Bryn Dewin Rangers was attracting more supporters at its home fixtures as they racked up consistent wins. Now in their highest position for many years, winning the league title was a distinct possibility, and Bryn was regularly in the team with improving performances.

He grinned as he relived the moment when he scored the winning goal. No vision of an absent father troubled him this time. He swerved past a defender and neatly flicked the ball over the advancing keeper's head. His teammates had hurled themselves on top of him in congratulation.

As he picked himself up, Bryn had glanced towards the touchline and seen familiar faces yelling their delight. It was great to see Granddad punching the air and Mum smiling proudly. Even better was seeing so many of his classmates at the match, including Carys who was screaming her support.

So much had happened since that awful, terrifying day at Wizard's Rock, thought Bryn. He opened his eyes to see Cadno at the water's edge, barking at two ducks swimming nearby.

Bryn sat down on the bank and grinned at the ducks as they quacked their annoyance, and continued swimming. Cadno eased his way down the bank until his feet were submerged, but was unsure about venturing deeper.

'But the best thing was after the match, Cadno. It was fan…fan-magic-tastic, when Bob introduced me to that guy from the Rams. Know what? He was a scout for 'em and knew Bob. He said real nice things about the way I played. Maybe, one day I'll play for Derby County.'

He looked round at the peaceful scene. Daffodils were in wild profusion everywhere, and the bushes and trees were alive with new greenery. What a different atmosphere in the village nowadays. It was happier. People smiled, and everybody at school was friends now, even Carys.

Her cave has been cleared out and the book burnt. Neither Carys nor any of her followers had ever returned. No one talked about Emrys Morgan or what happened on the Court of Foxes. It was as though that awful day had never happened, but there was still a reminder, a very weird reminder of Emrys Morgan.

Someone, or something, kept his grave tidy. The grass was cut, gravestone cleaned, and on the anniversary of his death on 7 December, a spray of mixed flowers was placed against the headstone. It was the talk of the village as everyone denied being involved, and no one was ever seen near the grave.

Bryn made his final entry in his secret diary and wrote, satisfyingly, The End. Now the story of his amazing, frightening adventures was hidden in a box in his bedroom.

He smiled as he visualised the vicar watching his congregation enlarged each Sunday, a beaming smile on his face.

Christmas had been a particularly happy time. It wasn't just the heavy snowfall, transforming Morredin into a fairyland, but the church had been full on Christmas Eve. That was the only time Bryn had gone back to a service. Afterwards he had admitted to grandfather it had almost been fun, with the lusty singing of carols.

He wandered back to the altar-like stone some weeks later. All the ashes of his teacher had blown away, and the police were puzzled why Hugh Price just vanished without telling anyone, or leaving a forwarding address.

Anwen Hughes was now in charge of the school, and a replacement teacher was expected who liked soccer as well as rugby, much to Bryn's approval.

Idris climbed the hill, following directions given by Bryn. When he reached the opening of the cave, he could see that is was blocked with tons of rock, following the earth tremors of that fateful day.

Bryn turned round and looked at the Court of Foxes. The twin peaks shimmered in the sun and looked less menacing. Since the demise of Emrys Morgan, he had not seen any foxes, and his nightmares never returned.

In fact, thought Bryn, as time passes I wonder sometimes if it wasn't all a nightmare. But then Selwyn is real, and I'm glad granddad and the vicar realise he was always a good person and on their side. But he still doesn't go to church.

He looked up as a familiar figure approached.

'You have much on your mind, Bryn. I see it in your eyes.' Selwyn chuckled as he sat down by his young friend. 'I seem to remember I said something similar when we first met.'

'Just thinking,' said Bryn. 'So much has happened since…'

'Since we defeated evil in this village, ' Selwyn beamed.

'Made a good team, didn't we?'

'What are your plans now?'

'I am glad I've found you, my young friend,' said Selwyn, and sighed.

'Why?'

'Because I journey to Scotland. I am hearing stories of evil visitations on one of the outer islands.'

'But you can't go,' cried Bryn.

'I have to go where my voice tells me. Sadly, I am not a free spirit, but have a mission in this life to fight evil wherever I find it.'

'So when are you leaving?' said Bryn, crying quietly.

'Tomorrow. Let us give each other a final hug and part now. I hate goodbyes, especially with such a special young friend like you.'

Bryn stood up with Selwyn and hugged the old man tightly. Tears tumbled down his face as he felt the strong arms round him.

'Now I must go,' said Selwyn, gently pushing Bryn away.

'Mi-the-a-een,' stammered Bryn, his brow furrowed in concentration.

'I think you mean 'mi fydda i'n dy golli di," said Selwyn, and smiled. 'I'll miss you too, Bryn.'

'Will I ever see you again,' shouted Bryn as Selwyn disappeared over the top of the bank.

Only the cries of the birds and the babble of the stream answered.

END

AUTHOR'S NOTE

This book is based on the true story of Dr John Harries, a wizard, whose powers were legendary in a small village in Mid-Wales. He died in 1839, but there exists a photograph of him in the National Library of Wales. It was taken when such a photograph should not even exist. The book of seven locks existed, and the split 'Harries Stone' can still be seen in the hills.

Welsh regional winner of the 2006 Undiscovered Authors novel competition, Brian Lux has previously published articles in many journals and magazines, ranging from professional to animal, yachting and a Boy's Annual. He has also enjoyed success with short stories and the occasional poem. His first childrens' book, Loppylugs And The Dam, was published in 2007.

Enjoyed this book?

Find out more about the author,
and a whole range of exciting titles at
www.discoveredauthors.co.uk

Discover our other imprints:

DA Diamonds traditional mainstream publishing

DA Revivals republishing out-of-print titles

Four O'Clock Press assisted publishing

Horizon Press business and corporate materials